Don't Go to Sleep

Billie Dureya Shell

DON'T GO TO SLEEP

Front Cover Image By grafic designer Billie Dureyea Shell & Kenny Writes

First Printing Edition 2020

ISBN 9781735023410

This book is dedicated to:

My son Ant' Juan D. Shell, I love you son
this one is 4 you.......

Acknowledgement

Once again I want 2 give thank 2 God for this gift I am so grateful for him giving me away 2 provide 4 my family in my house we will alwayz put you first.

To my mother Mclessie Shell you taught me so much and you loved me NO MATTER WHAT I love you so much momma.... What's up on with some bake chicken LOL😊.

To my little sister Glenda I love you and miss you blackie get at ur big brother Lil Sis.

To my Wife Shatoya Shell you get on my damn nerves but I wouldnt trade you 4 anything In the world I Iove you more then words can ever express.

To all my children I love y'all Jazmine, Ant'Tuan, Davon, Anthony, David, Lil Dureyea, Alura, Queen Diavion, Cameron, Preniece, Shaniece and Tajh I love u all and I'll 4ever have ur back you all give me a reason 2 smile.......... to my cousin Zane RIP nigga I miss u more then anyone will ever no, your always remembered love you bro.

To my cousin Ty I miss you thank 4 looking out 4 me and Zane you played a big part in my life and I always looked up to you l love you... Uncle Woody I miss you and love you, you no your my favorite uncle....

To my nigga Jamal love you, my brothers Lawrence and fred thank 4 showing me the game I love yall 4 that.

To my oldest sister Nedra love you thank you 4 always having my back. to my family uncles anties cousins etc.. I love y'all even those of you that act funny as fuck

To my dark side niggas y'all no what it is YAAH GANG........

Now to all my readers and fans I love you thanks for reading I hope u enjoy this book as much as I enjoy writing them with this Corona Virus 19 shit there ain't shit to do but write so I'm on my shit with that being said y'all be safe cover your face and love each other life is short so love the ones that really love you I'm gone enjoy the book.

Merry Christmas

Author

Billie Dureyea Shell

Chapter 1

DECEMBER 7

The Armstrong family, though young, had a tradition of decorating the house for Christmas on the first Saturday of December. Little did they know the terror waiting on the other side of the holiday season of 2020. Decorating was an all-day event. Brandon Armstrong started his morning at seven o'clock, dragging the creaky old ladder from the garage to hang an array of lights and an inflatable Santa Claus to overlook the neighborhood from their rooftop. His muscles were loose, ready for the treachery ahead. Brandon was by no means a physical prodigy, but managed to keep himself in healthy shape. He had hazel eyes and black hair that formed a subtle widow's peak his wife liked to play with when they lazed on the couch in the evenings. He and his wife, Erin, had come a long way since life as an engaged couple in a small townhouse eight years ago. Those times were much simpler, with only two windows to decorate in addition to a skinny Christmas tree. Erin seemed to add more decorations to their growing collection every year, turning it into a demanding annual project. While Brandon spent the first two hours of his day on the roof, Erin remained inside with the kids, keeping them entertained with Christmas movies, coloring books, and toys, all so she could pack away any visible non-Christmas decor. Even the kitchen had to be remodeled with Christmas-themed dishes and silverware, placemats, and Santa seat covers. By the end of the brutal day, it looked as if the North Pole had vomited all over their home. They reached this point of the night, a few minutes past nine. The kids were in bed, and Brandon and Erin were relaxing on the living room couch, admiring the completed Christmas tree.

The smells of the evening lingered: freshly baked cookies and a newly lit peppermint-scented candle to further enhance the festive mood. As much as Brandon found all of this absurd and unnecessary, the first night of the holiday ambiance always put Erin in the mood. After the kids had fallen asleep, she slipped into her Mrs. Claus lingerie of red silk panties and a red velvet top with fuzzy white trim that ended just above her belly button. She wore a matching Santa hat, letting her wavy ginger hair flow freely below it. They enjoyed a drink together, Erin sipping from a Frosty the Snowman mug filled with rum-spiked eggnog, while Brandon tended to a glass of scotch. "Another year in the books," Erin sighed as she leaned on Brandon's shoulder. She looked up to him with her big brown eyes and lightly freckled face. "The house looks great," Brandon replied. "As always." It was far from another year in the books. There was still gift shopping, visiting family, and trying to keep the kids from turning into spoiled brats after the barrage of presents they would receive. Brandon looked forward to December 26th when all of the drama would finally come to an end, then again to the first Saturday of January when they spent another day returning their house to normal, sending Christmas back into storage where it waited another eleven months to return. "I got us something new this year to try with the kids," Erin said, rising from the couch on her thick, gymnast legs. She dashed into the kitchen, the sounds of cupboards opening and closing. Her feet whispered along the hardwood floor as she returned, a doll the color of wheat toast clutched between both hands. She held it up like an ancient relic, a smirking elf dressed in green tights looking at Brandon with a crazed stare, one plastic eyeball fixed on him, the other pointed toward the ceiling. Nemo, the family's brown Dachshund, whimpered at the sight of the doll and cowered under the Christmas tree. "What the hell is that thing?" Brandon asked, a crooked grin spreading across his face. "He's an Elf on the Shelf doll I picked up at the thrift store." Nearly all of their Christmas decor had come from the damn thrift store, so it was no surprise for Brandon to hear of this latest purchase. "I thought those elves were supposed to wear red and look cute. Not this raggedy thing." "It doesn't matter what the elf looks like, as long as it's an elf we can move around the house. Just think of all the fun we'll have with the kids." "The kids? I've seen what adults do with these dolls," Brandon said with a chuckle. "Set up the elf for an orgy with naked Barbie dolls. Have him passed out on the counter with empty booze bottles around him. I just might have to try and get a laugh out of you." "Don't you dare let the kids see him doing anything raunchy," Erin snapped, fighting off a smile of her own. She waved the elf in the air as she sat back on the couch next to Brandon. "He's kind of creepy-looking, don't you think?" Brandon asked. Erin smacked him in the arm. "He's cute!" She shoved the doll in Brandon's face, the elf's graycrooked eyes staring in every direction, its pointy red hat flopping over its dark brown hair made of yarn. Its body and outfit were clearly made from an old felt that trapped the musty smell of its history, pleasantly arriving in their living room. "If you say so. What do we do?" "It's easy; we just move him every night to a different place in the house. Have him do something new. The kids wake up and have to find him. His story is that Santa sends him to keep an eye on the kids and report back if they've been naughty or nice." "Again, creepy." "Oh, B, it's for the kids, and they won't think it's creepy. They're gonna love him! Speaking of, they'll need to give him a name tomorrow morning when he 'arrives' for the first time. So start thinking of Christmas names that we can suggest." "It's hard for me to think of anything with you lying next to me in your outfit. Maybe we can let the elf know we've been naughty." Brandon tipped his mug back to finish his alcohol while Erin giggled. "If you keep making fun of the elf, maybe he'll be the only one who gets to see what's underneath." "I'd like to see him try." Brandon leaned in, Erin lying back as she tossed the elf aside to wrap her arms around Brandon's broad shoulders. Nemo let out another whine, but it fell upon deaf ears. They would remain on the couch for the next hour, their clothes piled on the floor, the elf's sideways stare locked on them the entire time.

Chapter 2

DECEMBER 8

Brandon woke the next morning because of a little girl's giggles coming from down the hallway. The bedrooms were all on the house's third level. For a Sunday morning, the sunlight remained rather dim, the clouds outside growing thick as they prepared to dump feet of snow on the Denver area over the coming weeks. Riley, their four-year-old daughter, was finally learning the practice of leaving Mommy and Daddy alone on weekend mornings, letting them sleep in a few more minutes than normal while she played with toy ponies in her bedroom. This peaceful routine only worked until their two-year-old son, Jordan, woke up and immediately started fighting with his sister, ripping the ponies from her hands and throwing them out into the hallway with an evil snicker. This always led to Riley whining, followed by her smacking Jordan and causing an emphatic wail. This particular morning was no different, and after their heated exchange, both kids ended up in Brandon and Erin's bedroom, yanking Brandon out of bed to pour their cereal for breakfast. Riley grabbed his arm with her tiny hands, pulling until he swung his legs over the edge. The kids were spitting images of their parents, Riley resembling her mother with light red hair and brown eyes, Jordan a miniature version of Brandon with his dark hair, hazel eyes, and the early hint of a prominent jaw beneath his chubby cheeks. He led them downstairs, groggy and bleary-eyed, as they chirped around him with a morning energy he could never reciprocate. They reached the main level and turned into the family room where the TV was turned on, showing Brandon's favorite holiday movie, Christmas Vacation. "Erin, you left the TV on all night!"

he shouted upstairs, receiving an exhausted moan in return. The elf sat on the couch, the TV remote at his side as he smirked that creepy half-smile. "And you did it for the elf? Really?" "Daddy, what's that?" Riley asked, stepping up to their new holiday family member. A sticky note lay at its side, and Brandon snatched it up to read. "Hi kids, I'm Santa's special helper all the way from the North Pole. I'm here to let him know if you've been naughty or nice. Give me a name and we can be the best of friends. And don't forget the most important rule: don't touch me, or else I lose all of my magic!" Brandon was probably supposed to read the note with a bit more enthusiasm, but he was tired and had no way to muster the energy for it. Heavy footsteps hit the ceiling above them, Erin jumping out of bed and running down the stairs. "Wait!" she yelled, entering the family room as she fastened a robe over her body. She crouched down to meet the kids' eye level. "I thought I heard little footsteps on the roof last night. This is our new elf – what do you think?" Erin did have the energy to radiate her excitement for their new elf, and this immediately riled up both kids. "Santa elf," Jordan said, his vocabulary still growing by the day. "Mommy, he said we need to give him a name," Riley said, matter-of-fact, batting her long eyelashes. "I heard. What do you think we should name him? Think of Christmas words." Riley pursed her lips as she entered a child's version of deep thought, counting the millions of possibilities on what to name their elf. "I know!" she cried out. "Snowball!" Erin grinned. "That's a perfect name, I love it." "S'owball," Jordan repeated, gazing cautiously at the elf on their couch, his thumb returning to its comfortable spot between his lips. "Hi, Snowball," Riley said, leaning on the front of the couch for a closer look. "Don't touch him, or else he can't fly back to the North Pole to tell Santa that you've been a good girl." "So he's going to sit in the middle of the couch all day on a Sunday while we're home?" Brandon asked, rolling his eyes. Sundays in the winter were for drinking booze, eating pizza, and watching football. Now he had to share his space with a twelve-inch elf whose frozen, bizarre eyes stared in the precise location of the TV. "Think of him as your new best friend," Erin said with a giggle. "Well, I hope he's a Packers fan, or else he might get thrown outside." "No, Daddy!" Riley shouted, inserting herself between him and the elf. "No, Daddy!" Jordan repeated, not sure what was going on, but copying his big sister. "Relax, you two. Snowball will be safe and isn't going anywhere. Daddy is joking." Erin crouched down again to calm the kids. "Let's go eat breakfast and leave Snowball alone." She led the kids into the kitchen while Brandon settled into the open space to the left of the elf, out of its vision. He sat back and enjoyed the movie, his entire body aching from the hours of manual labor on the roof yesterday. Erin disrupted the mood by blaring Christmas music in the kitchen, a routine that would drive Brandon toward the brink of insanity with every note of "Jingle Bells" and "Santa Baby" chipping away at his mind. Riley sang along, learning the words to all the songs to add to the orchestra of noise that accompanied this time of year. It had become a skill over time to block out the sound of Christmas tunes, and even with plenty of practice, it wasn't always possible to completely ignore it. The next two weeks would be filled with it whether he was at home, work, or out in public. It was unavoidable, just like his new task of moving the elf around the house every night. He'd leave the stress for later, knowing a hot shower awaited to soothe his muscles before starting his Sunday football ritual for the final time.

Chapter 3

DECEMBER 9

Monday morning brought the start of a new work week, Brandon rolling out of bed at six to get ready for the day. He worked for a tech company downtown that specialized in maintaining benefits and payroll for small businesses. The work itself was a little dry, but he enjoyed the office environment with its alcohol cart, lax dress code, and beautiful location in the heart of downtown Denver. He didn't even have a set schedule, able to arrive as he pleased, opting to leave the house by 6:30 so that he could return home early enough to enjoy time with the kids before they went to bed. Erin worked at a preschool but didn't have to go in until nine. She continued her light snoring as Brandon slipped into his jeans, tiptoeing around their bedroom so as not to disturb a soul in the silent house. Once dressed, he shuffled down the hallway to poke his head into each kid's bedroom, blowing them a silent kiss and wishing them a good day, before returning to give Erin a kiss on the forehead. She always returned a half-mumble, half-moan, then rolled back on to her side for a final hour of sleep. Running a couple minutes behind, Brandon remembered that he forgot to move the damn elf to a different location last night. He raced down the stairs, his footsteps heavy thuds against the silence. He'd have to make it a simple move for the elf this morning, no time to figure out something elaborate, not that the kids would know any different. They were simply floundered by the little guy's magical abilities. Brandon swung around the corner into the family room and stopped himself when he found the elf not sitting on the couch, figuring Erin had moved Snowball before she went up to bed. He walked a lap around the main level, halting in the hallway that connected the kitchen to the front door entry. Normally on the hallway's walls hung a handful of family portraits, a mixture of memories of both their time before kids and with kids. Instead, the pictures lay on the floor, frames splintered apart, glass shattered in multiple directions. A wreath hung on the entryway closet door, and in it sat Snowball, his felt arms hugging the wreath's body, legs dangling over the edge as if sitting on a swing. And, of course, his crooked stare looking toward the hallway. Brandon studied the elf. Didn't his eyes used to look the other direction? he wondered, but he couldn't say for sure. He took careful steps down the hallway, a keen eye on the floor to not step on any shards of glass. All of the pictures had somehow landed face down, the black backside of the frames the only thing visible. Brandon flipped over one frame and an instant chill blazed down his back. The glass had shattered in long cracks that looked more like claw marks all running in the same direction, meeting in a small circle—like a bullet hole—over Brandon's face. It's just a coincidence, he told himself. There have to be a billion possible ways for the glass to crack, and this just happened to be the one combination for this picture. The photo was of him and Erin smiling with the Statue of Liberty standing tall in the background, a shot from one of their first trips together as a couple, a year before they got engaged. Brandon flipped another frame and found the same thing, only this one had a crack running to Erin's face, a chunk of glass missing right where her grin was. He reluctantly flipped over the rest of the photos, finding them all to have a similar pattern of various cracks leading to a family member's face. The ones with the kids disturbed him even more, their innocent smiles tainted by the sinister, seemingly intentional, rifts in the glass. "Erin!" he called up the stairs. "Can you come down here?" A moment of silence passed before the sound of bedsprings creaked, her feet hitting the floor with a heavy thump and continuing as she stumbled toward the stairs. "What's wrong?" she called from the top in a loud whisper to not wake the kids. "I'm not sure—all of our pictures are broken on the floor." Brandon stood at the bottom of the stairs and looked up as his wife slid into a robe. "What do you mean?" she asked, descending the steps. He guided her to the hallway where the remains lay scattered across the hardwood floor. "What the hell is this?" "I don't know. I came down and found it all like this." "Was there an earthquake last night that we didn't feel?" "I don't think so. There'd be more things knocked off the walls and shelves." "Are the other pictures still on the wall?" The other pictures she referred to were the ones hanging in the living room. Brandon hadn't checked, and at this point, was afraid to go look. He shrugged his shoulders, prompting Erin to pivot and go check for herself. "These ones are fine," she called out, Brandon sighing relief, not that it helped explain what had happened in the hallway. Erin returned with her arms crossed, eyes studying the mess on the floor. "Do you think it was Nemo?" "How could Nemo have done this?" Nemo slept on the main level and was currently the only witness to what had occurred last night. He snored on his bed tucked in the corner of the kitchen, next to the doggy door that led outside. "He must have been chased a spider or something right up the wall and knocked the pictures off. How else do you explain it?" "I mean, that's possible, but that sounds more like something a cat would do. I don't think dogs chase bugs, at least not to the point of trying to run up the wall. I'd think we would have heard all of that noise, too." "Not necessarily. When the heater kicks on, it's almost impossible to hear what's happening down here." Brandon stroked his face as he considered this. It was by no means a satisfactory explanation, but it was an explanation nonetheless. "I'm late and need to go," Brandon said, checking the time on his phone. "Yes, go," Erin said, waving him away with her hands. "I'll clean this up and we'll plan to get some new frames this weekend. Can you look at some of those in-home security cameras we've been talking about? I've been wanting some for months now. If we had them, we'd know exactly what happened last night." "Yes, of course. I'll see what I can find." He kissed his wife before rushing out of the house, Snowball the Elf the furthest thing from his distracted mind.

Chapter 4

DECEMBER 10

Monday had passed without further thought on the fallen pictures. Returning to the routine grind of the work week had a way of clearing the mind of anything significant, the drag and lull making the upcoming week seem like a never-ending marathon to the finish line of Friday evening. It wasn't until Brandon returned home for the night that he remembered what had happened in the morning, but the surprise had long since faded. Erin's theory now made sense, having stewed in his subconscious all day. Nothing else had been knocked off the walls in the house, and Nemo wasn't the biggest of dogs, so perhaps he did become a bit skittish at the sight of a bug. Even being home for the evening brought its own comforting routines. Brandon prepared dinner so the family could eat as soon as Erin and the kids arrived home at six, followed by bath time for the kids before bedtime. They then enjoyed a couple hours together watching TV and unwinding from the day, sipping tea or eggnog until Erin went up for bed at 10:30. "Don't forget to move Snowball," she said before ascending the steps. "The kids loved him in the wreath today." Brag about it, why don't ya? Before heading up for bed, he grabbed the elf and moved it to their kitchen table, propping it up in a sitting position against the napkin holder. Brandon scanned the area for a prop and found a small children's book, the kind made of cardboard and usually handed out as part of a fast food restaurant's kid's meal. He swiped the book off the floor, lost and forgotten under the lounge chair in the family room. Twinkle, Twinkle, Little Star was the book, a solid, dark blue cover with a grinning yellow star and owl floating in the sky. He opened the book and placed it in the elf's lap, adjusting his bulky cotton arms to give the appearance of reading. "Enjoy story time, you little creep," Brandon said with a chuckle. The elf gazed sideways toward the wall, looking nowhere near the book in its lap. Brandon turned off the lights and headed upstairs for bed. * * * Brandon jumped out of bed as soon as his alarm sounded. The events of the prior morning had made him late, and he vowed to not let it happen again. Once he was ready for the day, he kissed Erin and poked his head into the kids' room before running downstairs. There were no broken pictures on the floor, just a quiet house as normal. Snowball had tipped forward, face first, into the book, so Brandon sat him back up before leaving. The garage door hummed as it slid open, revealing a gray, dismal sky. Cold air whooshed inside, making Brandon shiver as he approached his car. The fresh smell of an upcoming snowfall filled his nose, and he prayed it would hold off so he could avoid shoveling the driveway when he returned home. He dropped into the driver's seat, tossing his backpack to the passenger side, and grabbing the car keys out of his pocket to turn on the ignition. Clickclickclickclickclick. The lights on the dashboard flashed, his car's way of telling him something was wrong, but unable to specify what exactly. He tried again. Clickclickclickclickclick. "Goddammit!" he shouted, punching the steering wheel and stepping out of the car. His first thought was a dead battery. He reached back in and pulled the lever to unlock the car's hood, shuffling around and throwing it open as rage boiled within. I actually got out of bed with my alarm, and now this shit happens?! Brandon rarely knew what he was looking for under the hood of a car, only hoping to identify something that appeared out of the ordinary. Everything seemed perfectly fine. The ground felt slick beneath his sneakers, and Brandon looked down to find a puddle of liquid oozing out from underneath the car. "What the fuck?" he whispered, shuffling his feet to dry ground, a trail of clear, shiny liquid following his steps. He squatted and dipped his pinky finger into the liquid for closer examination. He studied his fingertip, the liquid's color lighter than oil, and somehow slicker. He whipped out his cell phone, turned on its flashlight, and dropped to all fours, craning his neck for a view underneath the vehicle. He saw drips from three different areas, the liquids falling from frayed cables. The droplets gathered in the middle of the car before flowing like a river to the front where he had stepped in the puddle. "Someone did this," he said, jumping to his feet, fear swallowing his rational senses as he spun around, frantically searching for someone hiding in the garage. "Show yourself!" he barked, his voice echoing. The garage didn't have much space beyond the two cars it housed, but that didn't matter to Brandon. He walked laps around it, checking the corners and even the rafters that served as overhead storage space. Why would someone do this? His heart thwacked his ribcage, adrenaline pulsing in his fingertips as he anticipated someone jumping out and attacking him. But there was physically nowhere for someone to hide unless they were the size of a child. He dropped to the ground again, this time to check underneath Erin's SUV, finding the ground below her car dry as a desert in the middle of July. He rushed inside the house, slamming the door hard enough to rattle the walls. "Erin!" he cried out. "We have a problem." Again, he thought, briefly remembering the fallen picture frames. No movement came from the bedroom upstairs, so Brandon ran up the steps to find Erin undisturbed, an arm slung over her eyes to block the daylight. "Erin!" She moaned before rolling to her side, slow blinking as she woke. "Erin!" He nudged her arm, startling her into consciousness. "Someone cut the lines under my car. There's fluid all over the garage and the car won't start." She sat up, too slow for Brandon's urgency, and stretched her neck. "What do you mean someone 'cut the lines'?" "I looked, and they're cut. Someone did this." Erin rolled out of bed, still not as distraught as her husband. "I highly doubt someone broke into our garage, cut your lines, and left." "I know what I saw. I need to take your car to go get my stuff at the office so I can work from home." "I'm sure there's an explanation. Relax." Brandon's frustration reached a tipping point and he had to make a conscious effort to not unleash it on Erin. He checked the time and saw he was now running fifteen minutes late, again, and this time with no vehicle to get to work. "Just take my car, get your things, and I'll call a mechanic to come out and take a look." She spoke calmly as she embraced Brandon. Normally he was the one calming her down, but the roles had reversed on this flustering morning. "It's nothing that can't be fixed. Just breathe and it will all be fine." Brandon took a deep breath, feeling his nerves physically settle down. "Thank you." He gave her a kiss before leaving, a distant and subtle sensation growing within that suggested some horrible entity was personally coming for him. Something felt off, and not quite so coincidental about the events of the last two mornings.

Chapter 5

DECEMBER 11

B randon woke on Wednesday, reluctant to get out of bed. He made no promises of arriving early to work, and still had his computer should he need to stay home again. A mechanic had come over yesterday afternoon to repair the damaged lines, believing it may have been a raccoon by the looks of the chew marks. "You've a gap underneath your backdoor of an inch and a half," the mechanic had explained as he pointed to the door in the garage that connected to the backyard. "That's all a small 'coon needs to squeeze into a place. I've seen this plenty of times before; I'd suggest closing up that gap with a rubber strip. Won't keep out smaller creatures like mice, but they don't do damage like this." Brandon accepted the blame. The gap was one of the tasks on the ever-growing list of house chores that needed to be done since they moved in five years ago. A list that grew every week, but was prioritized on whatever was wreaking havoc at the moment. A rubber strip for the door now became the top priority after spending $700 on repairs to fix three destroyed lines. He felt sick swiping his credit card. An unexpected expense of this amount with two weeks until Christmas presented a new stress they didn't need. They hadn't even started shopping for gifts. Brandon had a Christmas bonus arriving soon, but it would now all go toward paying off this new debt. A fucking raccoon? he thought after the mechanic left, sulking in his pity. These joyous memories ran through his mind briefly when he woke up on Wednesday, curious as to what disaster awaited him today. The holiday season had stressed him out ever since Riley was born. On top of the horrendous Christmas music, he had to juggle shopping, family, in-laws, holiday parties he had no interest in, and wrapping those purchased gifts, usually the night of December 23rd. They seemed to have six different places to visit between Christmas Eve and Christmas day, and he longed for the day they'd get to be the ones staying at home while others visited them. Every day that inched closer to Christmas brought another steady drop of stress for Brandon, dripping gradually into his system as if he were hooked to an IV full of red and green chaos. The car troubles rushed this process, making him long for December 26th sooner than normal. He pushed these thoughts aside and got ready for the day ahead without a shred of enthusiasm. Wednesday was the halfway point in the work week, and getting over the hump always seemed the longest of days. He forgot to move the elf last night, and hoped Erin had done so, rushing down the stairs to see. Brandon stopped when he entered the family room to the sight of what appeared to be fake snow covering the entirety of the room. "What the fuck?" It was a whiteout, the floor mostly invisible, smothered by pure, white cotton. The couch and two armchairs were also concealed beneath the blanket of white. Nemo lay in his bed in the corner of the kitchen, watching Brandon with guilty, droopy eyes. The thick cotton in the family room dissipated as it trailed off into the kitchen, toward Nemo's bed where a dozen stuffed animal carcasses lay spread out in a semicircle around the dog. "Nemo, are you shitting me?" Brandon shouted. "Since when?" They had Nemo for a little over three years and he had never shown an interest in the kids' toys scattered throughout the house. He may have sniffed them on occasion, but never took one for his own pleasure. Nemo whined, curling his head into his body as he tried to shy away from the situation. Brandon pivoted to inspect the family room. "How did you even do this much? The couches and chairs, really?" He counted twelve different stuffed animals that had been gutted, their bodies nothing but shreds of felt and colored cotton. A pair of plastic eyes belonging to a stuffed monkey stared out from the rubble, watching Brandon as his anger levels elevated once again. "Three fucking mornings in a row with some bullshit. Unbelievable!" Erin's feet banged from above, her footsteps creaking as she came down the stairs. "Brandon, what's going on?" She froze when she turned into the family room, eyes bulging at the sight. "Oh, Nemo decided today would be a good day to destroy every stuffed animal in the house." His words dripped with disgust. "I don't even know how to go about cleaning this." Erin dropped her hands to her hips as she examined the situation. "I think we'll want to sweep first to get the big chunks out of the way, then vacuum whatever sticks to the ground." "And the couch. And the chairs." Brandon shook his head, arms crossed, his eyelids starting to twitch. "We're gonna find this shit coming out of the cracks of our furniture for months." "Just go to work and I'll take care of this." "Nope. I'm gonna work from home. Again. At this point, I'm terrified to leave the house. Something seems to go wrong the second I wake up, so I'm gonna stay here. I'm sure if I leave, my windshield will catch a rock, or maybe I'll get a flat tire." "Babe, you're being dramatic. It hasn't been that bad. Your car is fixed, the mess from the broken pictures is cleaned up, and this is the first time Nemo has done something like this. I've heard horror stories from friends who have dogs that do this every week." "I know nothing has been a huge deal, but it's a shitty way to start every single day. Made me late Monday, yesterday was a shit show, and now here we are today. If I go in I'll be late." He checked the time. "I'll still probably be late even working from home. I can't just let you clean all this by yourself." "Let's get started then," Erin said, crossing through the stuffed animal guts like an Eskimo trekking through a blizzard. "We have two brooms, it's really just the family room with a little bit in the kitchen." She pulled open the garage door and disappeared into its darkness to retrieve the brooms. For that brief moment as he stood alone in the family room, the house silent, the sensation of an invisible presence in the room washed over him. A shiver ran from his neck down his back, and the temperature seemed to drop in the room as if it was actual snow covering the floor instead of cotton. His gaze locked on the pair of plastic eyes, and he wondered if they once had a soul behind them. They didn't have the neutral appearance of a toy, and Brandon believed he saw life swimming behind its mindless stare. "Okay, let's do this," Erin said as she returned inside and closed the door behind her, two brooms in hand as she shivered. A draft of cold air wafted in behind her, and Brandon wondered if this was the temperature drop he had felt. He grabbed a broom and followed her lead as she started to sweep the mess. The cotton clumped into piles, but the broom bristles had no chance of scraping what clung to the fibers of the carpet, leaving a thin layer of what looked like frost on the lawn after a sprinkle of snowfall on a winter morning. "I know this is a stressful time of the year," Erin said. "But try to make the best of it. Laugh things off and don't take everything so seriously. Remember last year when Riley pulled down the Christmas stockings and ate all the chocolate? You were so close to getting upset, but look at how funny it is now."

"I know. I'm sorry, I just like things to go smoothly. This week has been a mess." And there's a new spirit living in the house, just come out and say what you really think is going on. He would never say such a thing to Erin. The idea seemed absurd even to himself, likely an overreaction. As they swept the family room, Brandon felt eyes watching him, and it wasn't from the plastic eyes that had already been swept away. Something was nearby, studying him, waiting for him. He tried to shake the feeling from his body, and it worked momentarily. Keeping his mind occupied helped, so he focused on sweeping, then vacuuming, maintaining small talk with his wife as they cleaned their house, their kids still innocent and sleeping upstairs. But those invisible eyes held their hidden stare, burning into his conscience where its presence would remain as the countdown dwindled toward Christmas.

Chapter 6

DECEMBER 12

Brandon supposed he might be going a little crazy. The lunacy of the holiday season had a tendency to make even the most laidback people snap under pressure. He often wondered why Christmas couldn't be more like Thanksgiving, gathering with family and friends to enjoy a meal and passing out from food intoxication. Why did Christmas turn the entire month of December into chaos? Christmas or not, the week had been turmoil for Brandon. While Erin was right about the incidents being minor, he believed something bigger was at play. The events were too random, and now too consistent, to brush off as coincidences. His mind flooded with a constant paranoia. Even while eating dinner with the family, Brandon kept his attention fixed around the house, waiting for something to move on its own, or perhaps hear a creaky floorboard while they all sat at the dining table. In bed, he tossed and turned, entangling the sheets between his legs while his body refused to find a comfortable position. The thermostat was always set in the low 70's during the winter months, yet a slick layer of sweat formed on his bare back, the sheets clinging to him as he flipped over every five minutes like a steak on a grill. Trying to clear his mind only led to more thoughts, falling down a mental rabbit hole that was only present in the middle of a difficult night. Erin snored beside him, oblivious to what might be taking place in their home. And that's what made it difficult for him to tell her his thoughts on the matter. There was no way to express what he believed without suggesting he might be losing his grip on reality. Besides, Erin handled the brunt of the Christmas preparation and didn't need to stress about anything further. Yet, Brandon felt it when he worked from home, alone in the house, but not feeling alone. It was more a sense of being watched. When he had stayed at skyscraper hotels in big cities for certain work trips, it sometimes felt as if he was being watched through the window where he stayed twenty levels above ground. Surely some dirty old man was across town in his own elevated room, watching through binoculars. With that thought, Brandon always closed the curtains before getting naked to climb into bed. He felt this same sensation as the clock approached one in the morning on Thursday. Someone's eyes were on him, and apparently no one else in the house felt it. His boss had told him to work from home for the rest of the week, but at this point he wanted to get as far away from the house as possible. His brain was a pile of dry brush, burning and itching with fatigue, eyelids swollen and heavy, and for a brief moment, the exhaustion won. All of the random fear had scattered away like chickens sighting a fox, and he dozed into a light sleep for the next four hours. * * * When he woke at five o'clock, Brandon's mind and body demanded he stay in bed. His eyes were puffy and bloodshot, his head heavy as if hungover, but the only thing he had drunk the night before was a tall glass of paranoia. The heater hummed, its white noise steady and soothing, and probably to credit for him falling and staying asleep. He had reached a point where he thought he could hear every single sound in the house, from the structure creaking as a gush of wind hit the exterior, to the distant wheezing from Nemo sleeping downstairs. The fact that he could work from home again meant he could sleep an extra hour. So he debated in his bleary, exhausted mind if the extra sleep outweighed another day home alone. Just sleep, he told himself. There's nothing haunting the house – you're just tired and jumping to irrational conclusions. Sleep will clear your mind. As he flipped back onto his side, his brain woke up and started having more thoughts. What's waiting for me today? No point in stopping after three days of fun. What will go wrong once I step out of bed? The curiosity swelled; he just knew something was going to go wrong this morning. Brandon believed in trends, and dammit, this ought to be a clean week of morning surprises. Part of him wanted to get out of bed and head downstairs to see what awaited. He would do a lap around the house, check inside the garage for any flat tires or fluid spills, see what Nemo was up to last night, and maybe make a gallon of coffee to get through what was sure to be a day from hell. Go to sleep, get another hour. And since you're working from home, you can take a nap on your hour lunch break, maybe even doze off a little early. Then you'll be all caught up. Brandon giggled, slaphappy as he lay next to his sleeping wife. He hadn't been caught up on sleep since Riley was born, fighting the good fight that all parents do in trying to squeeze in any few minutes of shut-eye they can steal. It was a struggle, but he eventually dozed off for a few minutes before waking to the sound of the shower in their master bathroom. The noise was distant as he remained many levels below full consciousness, but he was still alert enough to wonder why Erin was up so early to shower, and why she hadn't closed the door. Too tired to actually care, Brandon let himself remain under the tight grip of sleep. After what may have been ten seconds or twenty minutes—his sense of time a lost cause—he jolted awake when Erin reached over and nudged him. She also remained mostly asleep, not even opening her eyes as she mumbled, "You left the shower on." "No!" Brandon barked as if he had been wrongly accused. He lunged out of bed, balance slightly off, tumbling over a pile of dirty clothes he kept on the floor. "Riley?" he shouted as he raced into the bathroom, flipping on the light switch. Not only was the shower on and blasting at the hottest temperature possible, but scorching water blasted from the sink. Steam filled the bathroom, the sound of water droplets exploding on the porcelain shower floor. It had grown so thick that Brandon could barely see beyond three feet, while the humidity filled his lungs with a heavy dampness. He slid open the shower door to find no one inside. His first thought had been that Riley turned on the shower for whatever reason—who else would have done it? He flailed at the knobs, first turning them the wrong way before turning them off, and then reached across to turn off the sink, letting the bathroom fall into a steamy silence. Brandon grew dizzy after jumping out of bed so abruptly, his vision pulsing in and out of focus, heart pounding like a trapped animal in a cage. He dashed out of their bathroom and down the hallway to Riley's room where she snored, limbs spread in every direction. Across the hallway Jordan also remained asleep, though a bit more organized than his sister as he lay flat on his back with only his arms spread out at his sides. Who the hell turned on the water? Brandon's head had been ringing, but now started to settle, the sound of running water filling his ears. He remained frozen as he stood in Jordan's doorway, focusing his mind to figure out if the sound was real or simply an after effect of what had woken him. It's real. It came from the kids' shared bathroom in the main hallway. Brandon took slow steps away from Jordan's room and tiptoed toward it, the noise growing louder. The bathroom's light was turned off, and as he stood outside the open door, looking into the black hole, it became clear that the water was running from the sink. Legs wobbling with terror, he forced a confident step into the bathroom, flipping on the light switch and turning off the sink in one rushed motion. Just as in his bathroom, no obvious explanation existed as to what happened. The kids' bathroom had a bathtub behind a hanging curtain, so he pulled the curtain back out of instinct. The bathtub's water was indeed running, although at a slow, dripping pace. Drip. Brandon stared at it, brows furrowed, arms trembling beyond his realization. Drip. A small puddle had formed around the tub's drain where the droplets had fallen. It was hardly enough water to pour into the drain, a stream the width of a needle running from the puddle into the small, black hole. Drip. Someone turned on the water. Someone is in the house. Drip. Brandon couldn't take it anymore and turned the tub's knob to end the slow, taunting drip. He shuffled out of the bathroom and returned to the bedroom where Erin had somehow managed to stay asleep. "Erin, get up," he whispered. "What's wrong," she mumbled, rolling onto her back as she stretched her arms over her head, joints cracking. "I think someone's in the house." This got her full attention as she bolted upright, suddenly wide awake as if it had been lunch time and not four in the morning. "Shhhhhhh." Brandon pressed his index finger against his wife's lips to keep her from shouting. "Grab your bat and wait in the hallway outside the kids' rooms." They each kept a baseball bat between the bed and their nightstands. Erin kicked the sheets off her legs as she hurled herself toward the bat, snatching it like her life depended on it. Brandon shuffled around the bed to grab his. "I'm going downstairs." "Should I call the cops?" "Not right now. We don't even know if the person is still in the house. Let me go look." Brandon was terrified to have to head downstairs alone, but that was the price of being the head of the household. He'd have to sacrifice himself if it meant sparing the three precious lives upstairs. Tears ran down Erin's cheeks. "And get shot if he has a gun? No, I'm calling the cops," she demanded, flailing in the dark for her cell phone. "I don't want you going down there." "If someone was trying to hurt us they would have done it while we slept. The kids are fine and so are we—just let me go see what's going on." Brandon said this through gritted teeth, his nervousness clashing with frustration. Part of him believed there was no one in the house and there had to be a logical explanation for the running water. Why would someone go through the trouble of breaking into a home to turn on the shower and sinks? Perhaps they wanted to create a white noise upstairs while they robbed the main level. Surely turning on the water couldn't have been the objective of their trip. Thinking about it made Brandon feel violated. Someone had entered their home and walked up the steps while everyone slept, slipping into the bathrooms to turn on the water, and disappearing without a trace. He tightened his grip on the bat, growing determined to bash in the skull of whoever might be downstairs. His quivering legs stepped out of the bedroom and down to the top step. Erin trailed behind, bat gripped tightly and held high in front of her as she scurried down the hallway to plant herself as sentry outside of the kids' rooms. The staircase led down to an open landing beside the front door. To the left was the family room, to the right the hallway that had seen shattered pictures a couple days earlier, and beyond that, the living and dining rooms. Twelve steps separated the upstairs from the main level, and by the fourth step down Brandon had a clear view of the front door, closed and the lock bolted. Okay, so they didn't come in through the front. His mind raced, trying to figure out both how the intruder entered, and where they might currently be, his walloping heart the only audible sound. If they were trying to rob the house, then the back door made no sense. It would be too difficult to lug things outside and have to either hop the fence or run all the way around the house to the gate. The garage would be much easier for entry and exit. When he reached the third step from the bottom, the staircase's walls opened up, exposing Brandon like a sitting duck. Only he didn't fear being attacked, as he once again heard running water. His grip on the bat loosened, shoulders slumped, and he hurried the final steps until his bare feet met the coolness of the hardwood floor on the main level. All the lights were off, but he still managed to see the backdoor was closed, the blinds shut over the sliding glass door. And so was the door to the garage, closed and the lock bolted, just as they had left it before going up to bed. Nemo snoozed in the corner, undisturbed. The running water was clearly coming from the kitchen sink. Brandon flipped on the light switch in the family room to reveal an undisturbed space. Sweat slicked his palms and made for a slippery grip on the baseball bat Brandon supposed he no longer needed. It appeared no one had broken into the house, a fact both relieving and terrifying at the same time. His senses remained on high alert as his feet shuffled along the soft carpet of the family room toward the kitchen. He craned his neck for a view and saw the sink's faucet lever sticking straight up as steaming hot water spouted out. He lowered the bat and darted to the sink, turning it off. They had a bathroom in the hallway and he checked there as well. As expected, the sink was turned on, hot water only, splashing and making a mess on the counter top. He turned the knob off and racked his brains for any reason all the water in the house would turn on without anyone causing it to do so. He knew of power surges that caused the breakers to switch off, but was there such thing as a water surge? Perhaps a pipe burst somewhere in the city and sent an overflow of water to their house, forcing its way past the closed valves to create an early morning of chaos. It didn't sound possible, but he'd plan to look it up when his heart rate returned to normal and his mind could think clearly. With all of the water turned off, Brandon returned to the kitchen, swiveling around in search of anything that may have caused all of this. He found nothing. Nothing but the creepy elf sitting in the wreath that hung on the inside garage door. It was surely his overactive and flustered mind, but Brandon swore the elf was looking at him. Grinning at him in a way that no longer looked childish, but slightly evil. He brushed it off. It may as well have been a shadow he was jumping away from. "Erin!" he shouted as he started back towards the stairs. "Everything is fine down here." He rumbled up the steps, legs no longer shaking, the baseball bat a piece of wood again and not a deadly weapon. He reached the top landing to find Erin taking short steps away from the kids' rooms, her baseball bat still mounted in an attack position. "There's nothing down there," Brandon said in the most confident voice he could muster. "Not a thing. Nemo was sleeping, nothing was touched, all the doors are locked." Erin lowered the bat. "I don't understand. Who turned on the water?" Brandon shrugged. "I think this was some sort of freak plumbing incident. I'm not sure what else it could be. Nothing else happened besides the running water… I'll call a plumber later today and see what they think." Erin still had shock on her face, her eyes bulging but starting to settle back in to their sockets. "If you say so. And you're sure everything is okay downstairs?" Her eyes glanced to the stairs as if hell itself waited at the bottom. "I promise. Let's try to have a normal day and not worry about this." Brandon embraced his wife and kissed her on the forehead, the eyes and grin from the elf still burned into the forefront of his thoughts.

Chapter 7

DECEMBER 13

They made it through the prior day running on mental fumes, and after putting the kids to bed later that night, immediately went to sleep a few minutes before eight o'clock. He and Erin had shared a brief conversation before dozing off, Brandon explaining that it was perfectly plausible for water faucets to turn themselves on. There were actual cases of this happening due to water pressure adjusting during the cold winter months. Checking back, last night had fallen a few ticks below twenty degrees, cold enough for the strange phenomenon to occur. This explanation satisfied

Erin, although Brandon had stretched the truth. These occurrences were only possible when the outside temperature dropped below five degrees and subsequently rose above thirty the following day. Neither of these had happened, and Brandon still believed someone had to have done it. When Brandon woke on Friday morning, he found, much to his delight, that nothing had gone wrong in the house overnight. The elf remained in the wreath, so he moved it, sitting it up on the kitchen counter in front of the cookie jar, crumbling a chocolate chip cookie to make it look like Snowball had eaten it. The workday dragged for Brandon, as most Fridays tended to do, teasing him with the psychological finish line at the end of a particularly trying week. Even his manager, who had been briefed on the chaos, suggested he take the following Monday off for a mental day of recovery. Brandon thanked him, but he had no interest in staying home. Sitting around the house would only lead to his mind wandering down more dark rabbit holes. After a calm day at the office, he drove home with the music blaring, his mind still exhausted as the afternoon lull tried to hypnotize him to sleep. He even cracked his window to let in the cold air and keep him just uncomfortable enough to not doze off behind the wheel and become roadkill. They rarely cooked on Friday nights and pizza was often ordered. No cooking, no cleanup, no stress. He and Erin could arrive home and immediately relax. Even for a Friday night, going to bed at eight again sounded like the most tempting of offers. He hoped Erin felt the same. Brandon pulled into the garage, planning to use the hour alone for a quick nap before the rest of the family arrived, and skipped to the door with anticipation. With the garage door closing behind, humming as the wheels squeaked on the track, he pushed open the door and immediately froze. The knife rack on the kitchen counter lay tipped over, knives splattered across both the counter and the floor as if a bomb had gone off. Nothing else was touched aside from the knives. "What the fuck?" Brandon whispered, recoiling back into the garage, his hands shaking. He spun around in search of anything he could use as a weapon. His golf clubs stood in the corner, tucked away and forgotten during the winter months, so he ran over to grab his nine-iron before re-entering the house. "If someone's in here, show yourself right now!" Brandon shouted into the house, the only response his own voice echoing back. The kitchen table blocked his direct view of the middle of the floor where the knives lay scattered, causing him to crane his neck for a better look. He checked Nemo's bed to his right to find it abandoned, the vinyl flap over the doggy door pushed toward the outside. Brandon tightened his grip on the club's sticky leather as he moved into the kitchen. Not a single knife remained inside the rack. Eight steak knives scattered on the floor, some with the blades jutting upward from the pile that included a bread knife and a couple of Santokus. The big ones, the chef's knife and the cleaver, remained on the counter. Next to them were shears spread wide apart. The wooden block that held all of these lay on its side, empty, and only moved about an inch from where it typically stood. The elf remained in the same place further down the counter, yet Brandon felt that sensation again that it was staring at him, his fake grin silently laughing at him. "Fuck you," Brandon said to the elf, causing a nervous giggle to creep up his chest, leaving his lips as a gasp. He knew no one was in the house, and now wondered if his mind was playing tricks on him. "What's wrong with me?!" he screamed. Only it couldn't be his mind's doing—there was a physical pile of knives on the floor to account for. Someone, or perhaps something, had to put them there. "Did you do this?" he barked to the elf minding its business from the counter, cookie crumbs sprinkled over its lap like a toddler. Brandon chortled and shook his head, lowering his chin into his chest, his face rushing with the blood of embarrassment. "Look at you," he whispered to himself. "You're yelling at a toy." He looked back to see the door still open, letting out all the warmth, and letting in the frigid winter air. The furnace hummed on, as if mocking him for being so absurd. "A toy," he said again to assure himself of the fact, stepping back toward the garage to close the door. "I need a night of at least ten hours of sleep. And maybe a vacation." Brandon moved to the family room, golf club lowered to his side. His breathing was the only sound, minus a couple of creaks as gusts of wind blew over the house. He gazed at the spilled knives, waiting for them to stand up and start marching toward him, snipping at his ankles like a pissed off Chihuahua. "Everything has an explanation." Brandon spoke to himself, trying to calm his nerves. Could there be a spirit in the house? Brandon had watched plenty of TV shows and documentaries about ghost hunters, and they always seemed to be searching for a message beneath these types of random actions. He checked the knives to see if their pattern formed a message. Another step closer and he confirmed what he had been thinking all along: nothing. It was just a jumble of knives that had fallen off the counter. He checked the ones that remained on the counter, and again found nothing of significance. See, you're just paranoid. There's no such thing as this supernatural nonsense you watch on TV. That's why it's on TV and you never hear about it in the real world. Brandon tossed his golf club aside and sauntered over to the counter, standing the knife rack back up to its proper position. Not giving up his theory of an intruder, he checked the knives for marks or fingerprints, but found them clean, as if freshly washed. The blades scraped the counter top as he picked up the heavy knives and returned them to their spots on the rack. With the knife rack back in place, Brandon examined the counter for any other signs of movement. Something knocked over the rack, and there had to be a clue as to what it was. He found nothing, and even questioned the validity of the knives reaching the kitchen floor. The rack was positioned against the wall, two and a half feet from the edge, and studying the alignment made no sense. Brandon reached out a wavering hand and placed it on the backside of the rack, pulling it toward him, tipping it on its side. The solid wooden block rattled the counter with a heavy thud as Brandon took a step back to watch what happened. A knot immediately dropped into his stomach. As he feared, nearly all of the knives stayed in place. The shears did fall out in a slow-motion slide, like syrup oozing out of a bottle. Yet, they remained within two inches of the block and were nowhere near the counter's edge. The steak knives wiggled out of place, but remained in the block. The heavy-duty knives didn't so much as budge, solid in their slots, only to be removed by hand. "Fuck," Brandon whispered, scratching his head. The rack had not simply been tipped over. Someone—or something—either knocked it over with a lot more force, or tipped it over and pulled out the knives that ended up on the floor. Why the knife rack? he wondered. Why not knock over the cereal boxes, or the chairs, or open the cookie jar? Thinking of the cookie jar made his eyes dance back to the elf. If only its eyes were real and its mouth could speak, then Brandon might know what was going on in the house while he was away. The elf, with its crooked glare, had seen it all. Brandon stepped to it, crouching down and placing his elbows on the counter in front of the cookie jar. "It wasn't you, was it?" he asked Snowball. The elf didn't respond, as expected, although Brandon still harbored a buried fear that it just might open its mouth and start talking. Why, yes, Mr. Brandon, it was I, Snowball, it would say in a cheery, high-pitched voice. I was just trying to start dinner for you and had a little accident. I hope you're not too upset, I was only trying to help! Brandon imagined the little elf saying these words and howled laughter. His mind still raced with possibilities, but he tried to hear Erin's voice telling him that there was an explanation for everything. A raccoon had chewed his car lines, a crazed Nemo knocked the pictures off the wall, and a shift in water pressure caused all of the faucets to turn on in the middle of the night. And now, maybe it was an enlarged rat that ran along the counter and knocked over the knives? Yes, a rat. That's what we'll go with. The lie felt fake as soon as it formed, but it was better than the truth. It was believable enough to help Brandon pick up the knives and put them away. The lie pushed him through the rest of the evening, allowing a fabricated smile for the kids and Erin. The lie helped him sleep at night. The lie kept him sane, and that's all he wanted heading into the weekend.

Chapter 8

DECEMBER 14

Brandon long had the ability to lie to himself and pretend everything was okay. It was a process he had mastered during his adolescent years. First, he repeated the lie to himself at least 100 times, letting it play over in his head until it started to sound funny. Second, and most importantly, he had to keep his mind occupied. Any down time would let his mind wander, and wandering led to doubting the lie. Lastly, with the lie still fresh, he needed to go to bed and sleep away the truth. This allowed his brain to shut down, and by the time he'd wake in the morning, the line between truth and lie became even more blurred. Erin agreed that getting a good night's sleep on Friday night meant plenty of energy for the upcoming weekend with the kids. Monday was also the start of the kids' winter break, three weeks that Erin took off from work to stay home with them. Brandon had no issue falling asleep. He was still beyond fatigued from the week of interrupted sleep or early morning chaos. Erin was snoring before her head even hit the pillow, and within minutes Brandon dozed off, thinking about how he just might get more than eight hours of sleep, a rarity since becoming a parent over four years ago. The kids normally woke around seven on weekends, jumping on Brandon and Erin to wake up and feed them cereal, laughing as they did so. * * * They enjoyed nine hours of continuous sleep. The kids didn't wake up until 7:45, and even still, stayed out of their parents' bedroom. Brandon heard them giggling down the hallway, Riley whispering in her softest voice, Jordan copying her every word in between banging what sounded like a toy car against the wall and laughing each time. Erin had a knack for floating at a level just below consciousness, her eyes swimming behind closed eyelids as her brain heard the kids, but refused to allow her to wake up. Brandon remained half-awake, half-asleep, his head heavy as his eyeballs rolled back into his head, sleep reaching out for another grasp to take him back under for a few more minutes. Jordan banging on the walls kept him from falling all the way under, but he still enjoyed lying in bed with no physical interruption aside from his raging morning erection. When he fell into this trance, time became fuzzy. He had spent other mornings like this to see a whole hour pass, while others was only five minutes—even though it felt like an hour. This particular Saturday was one where they enjoyed the extra hour in bed, the kids' voices distant. It wasn't until Nemo started barking downstairs that woke Brandon all the way, his body seemingly glued to the bed in complete relaxation. The bark echoed throughout the house, traveling up the stairs and directly into Brandon's ears, causing him to moan as he stretched himself awake. Erin rolled over and folded the ends of her pillow over her ears like a teenager when their mom barges in to wake them up on Monday morning. The kids stampeded down the hallway, tearing into the bedroom in a cluster of laughs and giggles. "Daddy, it's time to wake up!" Riley cried out. "Time 'ake up, Daddy," Jordan copied. They ran to Brandon's side of the bed, and he kept his eyes closed to feign sleep, cracking them open just enough to see their grinning faces as they stood a whole twelve inches away from his face. Jordan reached out with his little fingers, jaw hanging open as he used great concentration to reach over and pull open Brandon's eyelids. Brandon could no longer contain himself as he burst into laughter, prompting more giggles from Jordan and Riley. "What are you silly monsters doing?" he asked, sitting up and swinging his legs over the bed. Riley grinned so wide her gums appeared larger than her teeth. Her hair stood in a static, frazzled mess. Jordan pulled his hand back and promptly placed his thumb in his mouth where he seemed to think it belonged. "Daddy," Riley said as if she was about to make a grand revelation. "Me and Jordan are hungry for cereal." "Bwekfess," Jordan said, his version of breakfast. "Yeah, I think Nemo is hungry, too," Brandon said, standing from the bed. Nemo had kept on barking, stopping suddenly when Brandon's feet hit the ground. A sharp thump came from downstairs, sending slight vibrations up to the bedroom, the sound like that of a bowling ball dropping on the slick lane. Erin bolted upright, hair in messy tangles just like her daughter. "What was that?" Brandon's heart immediately raced. It's the spirits, he thought. "I'll go look," Brandon said, hurrying out of bed, the kids still giggling at each other, oblivious to their parents' panic. He left the bedroom without grabbing his baseball bat, not wanting to spark any unnecessary curiosity from the kids. Besides, Nemo probably just knocked something over; he had been barking uncontrollably. Keep telling yourself that, that's good. Start the lie before you even see what damage is done. Nemo was barking and knocked something over, perfect start to another lovely lie. Brandon barreled down the stairs, his heart wanting to leap out of his throat. He nearly slipped on a step that would have sent him tumbling, but managed to keep his balance by squeezing the handrail. His feet hit the hardwood and he immediately looked left into the family room, saw nothing of significance, then looked right into the living room where the Christmas tree was toppled over on its side, a couple of ornaments shattered on the nearby coffee table. Nemo lay in the corner, his face buried into the ground as his tail wagged violently. Brandon immediately took this as a sign of guilt, not considering how a dog of Nemo's size could knock over a seven-foot-tall tree. "Nemo!" Brandon shouted. "Get outside right now!" He shot up a hand that pointed to the kitchen where the doggy door waited, and followed his dog toward it. Brandon returned to the living room to find a dark patch of carpet where Nemo had just cowered and pissed himself. "Goddammit!" "What's wrong?" Erin called from the top of the stairs, the kids snickering behind her. "Nemo knocked the Christmas tree over." Once the words left his mouth he realized how little the explanation made sense. Of course Nemo didn't knock over the tree. That would be like Brandon knocking over the massive pine tree in their backyard with nothing but his bare hands. "Don't worry about it, I'll get it cleaned up, it's not too bad. We'll just need to vacuum around it." The tree stand, though sideways, remained in the same location. Brandon squatted toward the middle of the tree and reached both arms into the thick, plastic shrubbery, the fake tree branches and bristles scratching his arms as his hands grasped the pole that held it all together. He nudged the tree, lifting it a couple of inches before his arms gave out and dropped it back to the floor with a quiet whoosh. The tree was much heavier than it looked, so Brandon planted his feet in the carpet and reset his grip before hoisting it upward with a loud grunt through his gritted teeth. He could barely move the tree on his own, so how was a dog a tenth of his size supposed to do so much as nudge it a centimeter? The tree stood back in its place, dozens of green bristles scattered on the carpet where it had lain. Brandon retrieved the trashcan from the kitchen and swept the shattered ornaments into it. Fortunately, none of Erin's specialty ornaments had been damaged, only a couple of the basic shiny balls that graced almost every Christmas tree in the world. Erin ran down the stairs, the kids tiny footsteps trailing behind her. "You sure you don't need any help?" "It's fine. Nemo is outside now. I just need to vacuum up these bristles and clean where he pissed on the carpet." Brandon nodded to the corner where Nemo had marked his territory. "What's gotten into him lately?" Erin asked, putting her hands on her hips as she studied the Christmas tree. A few ornaments had been moved out of place, but she could adjust those later. "First the stuffed animals, and now this. Maybe we need to take him in to get looked at." I'm sure it's all the Christmas music making him suicidal, Brandon wanted to say, but kept his mouth shut and smirked instead. "I don't know," he eventually said. "I'm sure he's just stressed because he hasn't finished his holiday shopping yet." This earned a chuckle from Erin as the kids wandered off to the family room where their pile of toys awaited. "Go start the kids' cereal and I'll finish cleaning up this mess." Erin offered a lopsided grin before turning to the kitchen. Brandon's lie worked. He had already convinced himself that Nemo had somehow knocked the tree over. He finished cleaning up the mess, ready for a relaxing weekend with the family, unaware of the hell that awaited him before Monday would arrive.

Chapter 9

DECEMBER 15

Brandon didn't let the tipped-over tree eat away at his mind like the events earlier in the week had. His shift in attitude helped him relax during the weekend. They had spent most of Saturday at home, not going out until the evening to see the Christmas lights display at the downtown zoo. The kids grew hypnotized with the displays, lured into a trance until they were able to meet Santa before leaving. Sunday passed quietly, a heavy snowstorm starting to dump after noon, keeping Brandon glued to the couch to watch football while the kids scattered their toys across the family room for an inside day of fun. Erin lay on the couch most of the day, falling in and out of naps depending on the kids' noise level. She had also kept Snowball alive, moving him both Saturday and Sunday morning, first to dangle off the front door's knob, as if he was trying to leave, and secondly at the dining room table, where she also staged a dinner for him with some of the kids' toy silverware and food. Overall the weekend felt normal, and Brandon thought he just might make it to the new year with no more issues. By the time Sunday Night Football started, he had forgotten all about the drama of the past week, merely glad to be in the warmth of home with his family. The kids went down at seven, shortly after dinner, and Erin went up to bed at ten o'clock like most nights, leaving Brandon alone for another thirty minutes before he decided to call it a night. The game had ended, so he flipped through the channels in search of a movie already in progress to easily jump into, settling on Bad Santa. He laughed the next half hour away as Billy Bob Thornton made a mockery of Christmas, and clicked off the TV at the first commercial break. He scampered around the main floor, making sure breakfasts and lunches were ready to go for the next morning, and that Nemo had enough food in his bowl. As he zipped up his work backpack, a piercing screech blared from outside, ending with the violent crunch of metal, much like someone stepping on an empty soda can. Brandon immediately recognized it as a car crash and dashed across the family room to the windows that faced the street. Holy shit! he thought as he peered through the curtains. Their house was on the corner of a four-way intersection, and a fire hydrant stood on the edge of their lawn, on the corner nearest the street. A car was smashed against the hydrant, its entire front end condensed as the back wheels lifted a couple feet off the ground. The hydrant blasted a fountain of water into the night sky, landing on the snow-covered lawn and road, creating an instant sheet of ice as the temperature had fallen below twenty degrees. Brandon couldn't see much else aside from the car being a dark color, so he raced upstairs to slip into his shoes. "Someone crashed into our yard," he barked at Erin, as she had already been sitting up. "Into the fire hydrant—you should probably call 9-1-1." "Are they okay?" she asked, jumping out of bed and swiping her phone off the nightstand. "No idea—doesn't look good from here. Just call for an ambulance." Brandon wasted no more time trying to explain an incident he hadn't even witnessed, and scrambled back down the stairs, grabbing a jacket from the coat closet, and barging outside. The snow that had fallen all day was light and fluffy, making no noise as he walked over it, leaving a trail of footprints as he darted across the front lawn, stopping ten feet from where the water had started to turn to ice. "Are you okay?" he shouted to the car. The windshield was shattered, a thick white circle appearing in the middle and webbing outward, making it impossible to see through the thousands of cracks. The car's engine puttered before it eventually died, leaving the lone sound of water spurting from the tipped hydrant. The water melted the snow that had collected on the lawn, revealing the brown and yellow remains of grass that had fallen dormant for the winter, seeping into the ground and forming a puddle that grew across the lawn with each passing second. Brandon noticed the water approaching his feet and turned around to go down the driveway and along the sidewalk for a better view inside the crashed car. Sirens sounded in the distance—the fire station was only across the neighborhood, a quick thirty-second ride to the house. The water flooded not only the lawn, but also the street and sidewalks, a thin sheet of ice forming beneath the constant flow. The night was pitch-black, the nearest street lamp across the intersection and not providing any visibility for Brandon. He slid his feet along the ground, arms splayed out to keep his balance, and moved toward the car where he saw the figure of a person through the driver's side window, face down on the steering wheel. "Hey! Can you hear me?" Brandon moved cautiously to not end up on the ground. The figure didn't budge, and Brandon immediately thought the worst, sparking a fresh wave of panic as he scrambled for the car's door. The vehicle was already drenched in water, the door slippery as he clawed to pull it open, praying the driver left the doors unlocked. Once he found his grip, he tugged and filled with relief as the door swung open. The figure was clearly a man: short hair, stocky build. But Brandon couldn't make out much beyond that. Blood caked his forehead, appearing black in the darkness, streaming down his face like tears. The man's eyes were open but smeared in blood, his jaw hung open, and his whole body leaned into the steering wheel due to the car's angle. Brandon's body shuddered, and he wasn't sure if it was the freezing temperatures or the fact that someone had died on his front lawn. He supposed it was a bit of both. A firetruck's flashing lights appeared around the corner, strobing and bouncing off the undisturbed houses as it came down the street. Did no one else hear this? Brandon wondered. It had only been 10:30 when he noticed the collision. Surely the entire neighborhood hadn't gone to sleep yet. The spewing fire hydrant died down as the firetruck pulled up next to it, six yellow uniforms jumping out, their boots clapping on the frozen pavement as they approached the smashed car. "Good evening, sir," a fireman said, leaving his group to speak with Brandon. He had a thick black beard, and stern expression stuck on his face, his fire suit reflecting the little light available. "Any idea what happened here? Do you know this person?" Brandon shook his head. "I don't. And I don't know what happened. I heard a loud crash and ran outside to this." The fireman nodded, looking over his shoulder as his team pulled the body from the vehicle and lay the man on a gurney. A woman hovered over him, pounding his chest with her hands as she performed a desperate attempt of CPR. The others gathered around, watching with their shoulders slumped, their heads to the ground. Brandon read their body language and figured the man had no chance of survival. The woman continued her attempt to resuscitate him for another two minutes before she took a step back, shaking her head. "Search the body and the car for any identification," the fireman who was talking with Brandon said to his crew. "We need to notify next of kin. Then we'll have to move this car so we can fix the hydrant. Dobbs, will you please call a tow truck?" One of the other firemen nodded and dashed back to the firetruck. A police car and ambulance rounded the corner and crept up to join them. Brandon would spend the next half hour repeating his statement to the police, and then again to curious neighbors who had finally put on some clothes and come over to see what had happened. Brandon fell into a state of shock as he stared at the dead body on the gurney. He saw a wedding ring on his finger, and prayed no kids were being left behind. The dead man's eyes bulged from their sockets, his jaw stuck open, looking like a petrified cat. Brandon watched as the paramedics zipped up the pale body in a black bag. By the time the commotion ended and the emergency vehicles pulled away, it was a few minutes before midnight. Brandon returned inside, his body a popsicle, but he was too numb to notice, too stunned to even consider complaining after witnessing such a horrific scene. A man died on his front lawn, but even more frightening was that he crashed into the fire hydrant. If the man had managed to swerve around the hydrant, the car would have easily burst into the house, into the family room where Brandon was closing up for the night. This night could have ended a lot worse, he thought as he pulled the frozen layers of clothes off his body. Erin had slipped into a bathrobe and paced the main floor while Brandon was outside. "He's dead," Brandon whispered to her. Erin shook her head, lips pursed as if wanting to say something, but not sure what to say. Instead, she pulled him into her embrace, rubbing his back in an attempt to warm his body that had little effect. All he could see was the dead man's frozen face, his eyes staring blankly into the abyss. Even though he was exhausted, lying down in bed was now the furthest thing from his mind. Erin stayed with him on the couch, eventually dozing off as she flipped through the channels. She had tried to lighten the mood with small talk, but Brandon could only manage short, one-word responses. He eventually nodded off at three in the morning, his mind blurred with commotion and fear.

Chapter 10

DECEMBER 16

Brandon called in to work shortly after his alarm sounded. He didn't remember it, but they had both made their way upstairs to bed at some point in the early morning. His brain prickled with fatigue, his bloodshot eyes heavy boulders in his face. He had no interest in functioning on a whole three hours of sleep. He told his manager what had happened last night and was promptly told to stay home and rest, take a couple days if need be. He expected something to happen in the morning, perhaps additional follow-up from the police department. Surely a man doesn't die on your front lawn and it simply ends with his dead body being taken away. But nothing happened. Such is life, everyone moved on. It was a car accident with no eyewitnesses to the actual incident. What more could Brandon offer if someone did show up? The hydrant had been repaired, and there was no damage to their property, the only remnants being two skid marks leading up to the edge of the lawn. Brandon wanted to know who the man was. Where was he going? Did he live in the neighborhood? Why was he driving so fast, and what made him swerve to his death on a deserted road? These questions picked at his brain, but once he saw Erin and the kids out the door, Brandon went straight for the couch, collapsing into a deep sleep. Riley had made a comment about Snowball being in the same place as yesterday, wondering why their little elf stayed put. Erin explained that he must have fallen asleep and forgot to move, an answer that Riley accepted, allowing her to move on with her morning. Brandon would move the elf later, having him in a new spot for when the kids arrived home. For now, he needed sleep and nothing more. The sun crept through the back door and kitchen windows, giving a soft glow across the house's main floor. Brandon momentarily debated going back up to the bedroom where the blackout curtains were still closed, but he had no energy to climb the flight of stairs. At this moment he could probably sleep in the middle of Bourbon Street during Mardi Gras. He dozed and was snoring within five minutes. * * * Brandon had no clue what time it was when he woke. The sun shined brighter from the back door instead of the front, meaning it was still before noon. He hadn't woken due to being rested—far from it, in fact—but rather a faint burning smell, as if someone had left a tray of chicken in the oven and forgot about it. He lay still at first, listening to the silent house for the sound of anything burning, taking deep breaths to make sure it wasn't a part of his imagination. The smell was definitely real, but remained mild, almost distant. No smoke filled the house, no burning sound to accompany the odor. He closed his eyes, figuring it was something outside, possibly a car's brakes—the stench was quite similar. A dull pop! came from the kitchen, followed by the rattling of the oven racks. Brandon jumped to his feet and dashed into the kitchen, off balance as his mind still fought to wake up. He had to blink the bleariness out of his eyes to see clearly, finding the oven was indeed turned on, the smell growing stronger as he approached it. "What the fuck?" Brandon lunged for the range, pushing the panel buttons to turn off the oven that had been set to the maximum temperature of 550 degrees. He pulled open the oven door, a blast of gray smoke pouring out like a campfire, choking him and sparking a cough attack as he raced around the kitchen to open the windows and back door. The smoke alarm blared to add to the chaos, the entire main level filling with gray clouds. He now flailed around to open every window on the floor, including the front door, which he exited for fresh air outside. His brain was still screaming for more sleep, rudely interrupted from the deep slumber he had been enjoying. The outdoors filled his lungs, clear and refreshing, sharp with its unforgiving briskness. Smoke oozed through the screen door, and Brandon saw it finally starting to clear out from the inside. After a couple of minutes passed, the smoke alarm ceased its screeching, and he returned inside, the burning stench still strong. He took slow steps as he re-entered the house, still unsure if the fire was contained, but assuming it was if the alarm had already turned off. The thick smoke had cleared, but there was still a thin, gray haze that reduced visibility in the entire house. Brandon reached the kitchen, keeping a safe distance, as he wasn't sure if the oven had turned itself on. Yeah, just like the water turned itself on, right? Inside the oven was a box-shaped object, completely black and charred, shriveling into itself. Embers glowed around its edges, but no longer had an active flame. Beside the box, a clump of green plastic clung to the metal rack, melted into near liquid and far from its original shape. Brandon recognized the specific shade of green as the bows Erin liked to put on the presents. He pulled open the drawer next to the stove and slid his hands into oven mitts, reaching out his shaky arms to the box and pulling it toward him with a hard nudge as it had become stuck to the rack. The exterior of the box was a total loss, unrecognizable, but what remained inside was still somewhat distinguishable, despite being burned and warped into a different shape. The object inside was a black and yellow toy tractor for Jordan to ride on. Brandon remembered Erin returning home with this after she had gone out shopping on Black Friday. Why was this in the oven? he wondered. He considered calling Erin, but decided not to, unsure what he'd even say. Hey, honey, Jordan's present was in the oven and someone decided to turn it on. Nothing like an oven-roasted tractor on Christmas morning, am I right? He giggled, still delirious with fatigue. They had gone the whole weekend—well, almost—without incident, but here they were again. Apparently the haunted spirit took weekends off and resumed its bullshit on Monday morning. Unless you've fully lost it, he thought. Perhaps you have a split personality doing things you don't even realize. One day at a time. You're going crazy. Brandon laughed at the thought, slamming the front door shut and running to the kitchen where he found the elf, its stupid grin mocking him. "You think this is funny?" Brandon barked, swiping the elf from the counter and pinning him to the wall, its cotton body squeezed in his fist. The elf vibrated in Brandon's shaky grip, and he swore its eyes were looking at him, looking into him. He hurled Snowball into the living room, its plastic eyes clashing against the wall before falling to the couch below. "Take a deep breath," he said to himself. "You're just tired and keep getting less sleep every night." He pulled out a trash bag, whipping it open to clean out the oven, and focused on clearing out the damaged present to keep his mind distracted, wondering how he'd explain this mess to Erin when she arrived home.

Chapter 11

DECEMBER 17

Brandon had decided to not tell Erin, and instead went to the store to buy another tractor, wrapping it and replacing it under the Christmas tree as if nothing had happened. The oven had cleaned out fairly easily. There were only a couple piles of ashes to clean up, while clearing out the burnt odor proved more challenging. He ended up having the windows open for an hour, not ideal on a day with high temperatures in the forties. The situation left him no choice but to clean the entire main floor. He could have cleaned just the oven, drowning it in a lemon-scented chemical cleaner as he had done, but that smell would linger as well, leaving more questions as to why he decided to clean only the oven on his unplanned day off. Shortly after tossing the burnt package in the dumpster, Brandon rode the only wave of energy he felt all day, breaking out the brooms, mops, and vacuum as he attacked the main level, spreading the lemony scent around the entire house. After two hours, he had finished cleaning, and his mind faded back to the deep fatigue that had grown familiar over the past week. Everything from his head to his arms and legs felt hollowed out by exhaustion. A task as simple as standing at the kitchen counter to figure out what to make for dinner proved too difficult for his current state, so he ordered takeout. Erin had no complaints about arriving home to a clean house, and volunteered to take care of the kids all by herself that evening, bathing them and getting them in bed so he could take another crack at going to sleep early. Brandon had explained it was another day of difficult sleep, it seemingly avoiding him at all costs the more tired he grew. Erin sent him out to buy sleeping pills, and he popped two at 7:30, asleep within twenty minutes, never seeing the other side of eight o'clock. It was a sleep so deep that he never felt Erin slide into bed beside him, didn't hear the TV play reruns of old 90's sitcoms. His body, not so much as a finger, never moved the entire time until he was woken in the middle of the night. It had been six straight hours of heavy sleep, respectable but not nearly what he needed, when his eyes shot open and he bolted upright. The only sound at two in the morning was that of the furnace humming as it pumped heat through the vents. The drugged sleep had him loopy upon waking, the room somewhat spinning, his ears ringing. Except, he did hear something. Something that pulled him up through all those layers of sleep. Something in my head? he wondered, focusing his hearing on the ringing silence. Brandon leaned over and turned on his phone screen to see the time of 2:03 A.M. Sleep still floated at the surface of his mind and he could roll over and be snoring within minutes if he wanted to, but a voice in the back of his head told him to keep listening. He closed his eyes with hopes of his mind shutting itself down, and even lay down on his stiff pillow, but he was already growing to accept that he wouldn't be sleeping again tonight, and he thought he might cry at the fact. Instead of sleep, his mind and ears focused on all of the nearly inaudible sounds that accompanied a big house in the middle of the night. From the faint creaks and moans, to the little snores coming from down the hallway, Brandon thought he might as well have been lying in the middle of an orchestra, the sounds filling his head in an amplified harmony, pushing him one step closer to a nervous breakdown. The night grew hot, the sheets sticking to his sweaty legs, so he kicked them down to his feet. Just then the heater kicked on again and blasted a fresh wave of warm air into the room, mentally suffocating Brandon as he rolled to another part of the bed where the untouched sheets were cooler against his skin. Why? he asked himself. Why does this keep happening? Am I so tired that my body can't sleep? Is this insomnia? He thought of the kids and how they could sometimes turn into screaming demonic monsters if they missed a nap or had a bad dream wake them in the middle of the night. They could grow so exhausted where all they wanted to do was scream, sleep an overlooked and obvious solution to the problem. And that's where Brandon found himself now, on the brink of screaming and shouting to wake up the whole neighborhood. To think he had been so close to a good night's sleep before that bastard crashed into his front yard. That one event had now thrown off a whole two night's worth of shuteye. His tongue turned dry, cotton-mouthed, perhaps from the sleeping pills; another annoyance to keep him awake. The thought of cold water splashing down his gullet sounded both heavenly and impossible. The idea of getting out of bed to drink a glass seemed the most daunting task at the moment. Instead he clenched his jaw and pooled up as much saliva as he could muster, gulping his own flavorless liquid down as it lay a thick layer over his throat. That's when the knocking began. It started so faint that he surely mistook it for bedsprings creaking in one of the kids' rooms. Then the sound elevated to a level that made him sit up again. He looked over to Erin who had remained undisturbed, chest rising and falling peacefully. The knocking wasn't constant, just a solid three knocks that may have been from a child's balled-up fist. Three knocks then fifteen seconds of silence. Brandon hadn't noticed this pattern at first, not until the fifth series when he started to mentally time the distance between knocks. Knock. Knock. Knock. A fresh wave of sweat beaded around his forehead. There is no knocking sound. It has to be in your head. Maybe one of the kids are flailing their arms around and hitting the side of the bed. Knock. Knock. Knock. Slightly louder this time, and becoming a little more clear that it was from the main level downstairs. The floodgates of paranoia opened and Brandon immediately returned to his thoughts of an evil spirit in their house, ready to terrorize the family while they slept every night. There is no such thing. Stop with the nonsense! Knock. Knock. Knock. "It's got to be a tree, something hitting the house because of the wind," he whispered to himself, both to create a new sound in the room and to ensure that he was actually awake. His breath tasted sour in his mouth, like he had sipped spoiled milk, confirming that he was indeed no longer in dreamland. It could be an animal trying to claw its way into the house. Maybe a fox or coyote. Knock. Knock. Knock. This time it was louder, sending slight vibrations up the walls of the house that he felt in bed. He shot a look to Erin to find her still undisturbed. His brain throbbed with exhaustion, yet his legs swung over the edge of the bed, feet dangling as he waited for the next set of knocks to echo their way upstairs. The sensation of someone breathing tickled the back of his neck, sending chills from head to toes as he jumped off the bed, muttering a confused, "Gahhh!" Not even his feet hitting the ground stirred Erin. She kept on snoring. Thump. Thump. Thump. Brandon spun around and faced the bedroom door. The sound of the knock became heavier, as if someone had switched from knocking with their knuckles to the side of a balled fist. Erin kept a set of porcelain figurines on the top of their dresser, and they danced and rattled at the intensified knocking. Brandon's heart banged in his chest, creating its own knocking within his head, his temples and jugular pulsing out of control. Thump. Thump. Thump. Brandon shuffled for the bedroom door, swinging his head toward Erin. She normally woke to the slightest of sounds thanks to her motherly instinct, but apparently someone trying to break down their front door wasn't enough to bring her back to consciousness. Thump. Thump. Thump. Brandon felt the vibrations underneath his feet as he stepped into the hallway and stood at the top of the stairs to gauge where exactly the sound was coming from. Fifteen seconds passed with silence. Then thirty. Then forty-five. He thought he was in the clear, pivoting toward the kids' rooms to check on them, when a sound so loud and sinister ruptured from downstairs, similar to someone hitting their house with a jackhammer. BAM! BAM! BAM! The pictures on the stairway walls rattled out of position, crooked like the times Riley decided it was a good idea to run her hand along the wall while descending the stairs. BAM! BAM! BAM! Brandon screamed, no longer concerned about letting his family sleep. Hell, he wanted them to wake up, but Erin still didn't budge, nor did any of the kids come running from their rooms.

BAM! BAM! BAM! The sound was no longer coming from downstairs, but instead from the walls in their bedroom. One of the porcelain figurines tip over with a clink! "Erin!" Brandon barked, running into the bedroom, diving onto the bed and over her sleeping body. "Erin, wake up!" He grabbed her shoulders with trembling hands. She moaned, licked her lips, then opened her eyes to find Brandon sweating and panting for breath. "What's wrong?" she mumbled, still clearly oblivious to what had been going on. "Are you shitting me? Did you not hear any of that? It sounds like someone is trying to break through our walls." Brandon pulled the covers toward him like a scared child afraid of the monsters under the bed. Everyone knew covering yourself was the only way to keep them from reaching out and snatching your ankles. "I didn't hear anything—" BAM! BAM! BAM! "Ahh!" Brandon shrieked, feeling the bed rattle as the vibrations filled the entire house. "What the fuck?!" "What's wrong?" Erin gasped, a sliver of annoyance slipping into her tone. "You didn't hear that?!" Brandon snapped, his jaw hanging as he looked to her.

"Babe, I think you had a nightmare. There are no sounds. You're clearly having some sort of aftershock from a dream." "No. This isn't a dream. I heard it. I felt it. Listen for it, I don't know how you can't hear it." Brandon put up his hand to call for silence, nothing audible but their breathing. A minute passed without another sound. "I told you," Erin mumbled and rolled back to her side. "It was a nightmare." Brandon sat in silence, waiting, heart racing, sweat dripping down his neck and back in cold streaks. I'm not going crazy, he thought. I know what I heard, and it wasn't any dream. Brandon lay wide awake as the clock approached 2:30 A.M., so he snatched his cell phone off the nightstand and Googled the possibilities of mental illusions when the brain lacked sufficient sleep. He would stay up for another hour reading, until he finally fell into a dreamless doze.

Chapter 12

DECEMBER 18

Brandon tossed and turned through the morning's early hours, and when his alarm sounded, he thought he might cry. He needed another day off from work—there was no way he could function after another long, horrific night. But the last thing he wanted to do was stay home alone again. I have to try. I need sleep. During the hour of reading, his mind had waited for more banging on the walls. He did learn that sleep deprivation had a direct link to both visual and auditory hallucinations. Lack of sleep can, in fact, lead to symptoms that mimic mental illness. Brandon had never felt so close to the brink of insanity during the prior night, even more so when Erin claimed to not hear any sounds. Sleep was the only solution. Deep, beautiful, undisturbed sleep. Half awake, Brandon sent a text message to his manager to inform he would need one more day at home. He didn't help get the kids ready in the morning, and Erin didn't ask. She had seen the crazed look in his eyes during the night and understood the dangerous depths to where her husband's mind was headed. She kept their blackout curtains closed, engulfing Brandon in near darkness, even as the sun tried to claw its way into the bedroom with no success. He slept right until noon, getting a solid five hours undisturbed and waking up naturally, no alarm, no crying kids, no haunted house. Sure, he was still tired, but his mind felt refreshed and able to form a clear thought. Hopefully the hallucinations were gone for good. Brandon remained in bed for another hour after waking up, basking in the dark silence, partly hoping he might fall back asleep, but gradually accepting that he was now awake for the day. His stomach growled, but he ignored it, enjoying the weightless feeling of having no responsibilities for the day ahead. The house was still clean from his cover up a few days earlier, and snow blanketed outside, leaving nothing to be done as far as yard work. He'd lay in bed until four o'clock, alternating between Netflix and reading books, and he did doze off for a quick nap at some point. At four, he rolled out of bed, got ready for the day—or the evening, at this point—and headed downstairs to eat a snack and prepare dinner. No haunted sounds, no tipped over knives, just a house how it was supposed to be in the middle of December with its Christmas decor setting a festive and joyful mood. He snatched Snowball off the counter and paced around the house to find a new place for him. He couldn't help but laugh as he looked at the toy elf with a clear mind, wondering just how close he had been to lunacy, like not knowing a shark is swimming twenty feet below you while you splash around the ocean. Brandon hung the elf on the top edge of the TV, making him appear like he was sneaking a peek at the screen. It was simple, but funny, and the kids would certainly get a kick out of their tiny elf craning to watch Paw Patrol with them. With Snowball settled, and Nemo snoozing in his bed, Brandon raided the kitchen for lasagna ingredients, ready to spend the next two hours crafting the perfect dish for Erin and the kids. It was rare when they had the time to make a tray, and it was always received as a special treat. Brandon played music while he prepared and cooked the food, dancing in the kitchen, singing and whistling along. He felt the best he had in a week. Catching up on sleep made everything that had happened seem insignificant, as if the fatigue alone had clouded his vision and made things a bigger deal than they were. He hadn't even thought about the dead man in his front lawn, and now believed Erin that he must have hallucinated the banging sounds. The kids arrived home with Erin, yelling in excitement when they smelled the lasagna in the oven. Brandon thought he inhaled a whiff of the burnt present, but chalked it up to his paranoid imagination. Life was normal again, and he had actual energy after putting the kids down for bed after dinner. He and Erin made love that night, and everything was right in the world. * * * Brandon had no issue falling asleep at ten o'clock, even though he had slept until noon earlier. His body was still likely a few hours behind on sleep and welcomed the chance to be completely caught up. The prospect of having a second consecutive day of feeling this sensational excited him. Even if, God forbid, something woke him in the middle of the night, he'd still be in good shape to head back in to the office in the morning, and finally get out of the house for a few hours. He slept soundly until midnight when the soft, yellowish glow of light kissed his eyes, making him see red insides of his eyelids. There's no way it's already the morning, he thought as he rolled to bury his face into the pillow. Impossible. He figured Erin must have gotten out of bed to use the restroom and refused to close the door like always. He reached an arm out and felt the warmth of her body still by his side. The light didn't fade, intensifying the more awake Brandon became. Brandon squirmed from the sensation, the brightness crawling on his skin like thousands of prickling ants. He rolled onto his back, eyes squinted shut as he clung to the dwindling hope that he'd get to fall back asleep. "Did you leave the light on?" he mumbled in Erin's direction, receiving no response. Brandon panicked, afraid he was having another episode of hallucinations. He shot up in bed, eyes wide, heart pounding like a drum. Not only was the bathroom light on, but so was the bedroom, the hallway, and the kids' bathroom. "What the fuck?" he muttered under his breath. "Erin, wake up." He nudged her, causing a drawn out moan as she attempted to open her eyes, snapping them back shut at the unexpected brightness. "What's going on?" she asked. "Why are the lights on?" "I don't know." Brandon rolled out of bed and grabbed his baseball bat. "Mommy? Daddy?" Riley called from down the hall. Brandon sprinted into her room, the bat hoisted over his shoulder, finding Riley sitting up in bed and rubbing her eyes, and keeping them closed from the blinding light. "Are you okay, sweetie?" Brandon asked, panting. "Why are the lights on, Daddy?" she asked, her voice stronger than his at the moment. He opened his lips to tell her he didn't know, but decided that might strike fear into his little girl. "I'm sorry, sweetie, Daddy was looking for something. Lay down and go back to sleep." He flicked off the light switch and watched as she tipped backward, moaning gibberish when she flipped onto her side and pulled the covers back over her body. Brandon stepped out and poked his head into Jordan's bedroom, finding his son sleeping upside down in his bed, an arm draped over his eyes to shield away the disrupting light. His little chest rose and fell as he continued his snooze. He turned off the light and returned to the hallway, turning off that light, leaving what appeared to be the rest of the main level below illuminated, judging by the glow from downstairs. "This is bullshit," Brandon snarled, a wave of rage consuming his tired mind. "Are the kids okay?" Erin asked. She had stayed in bed, sitting up with the sheets pulled up to her chest, eyes bulging with fear. Brandon stood in the bedroom doorway, his face turning red. "They're fine and sleeping. I have to go turn off every single light in the house now. Excuse me." Brandon stomped down the stairs, baseball bat resting on his shoulder. It's now been more than a week of these events waking you up every night. He reached the main level and puttered around like a madman, flipping off all the light switches until the darkness of midnight was allowed to return. A thin line of light glowed from beneath the door leading to the basement. "Goddammit! Really?" he barked as he pushed open the door and stormed down another flight of stairs, ready to snap. Fire filled his veins, and his brain felt like it was physically pressing against his skull in an attempt to break out. Oh, God, how he just wanted a night of uninterrupted sleep. "One fucking night, c'mon!" he barked into the basement, knowing no one all the way upstairs would hear him. Exhaustion grabbed hold, making his head feel like it might split in two pieces. The back of his eyeballs itched, and he wanted nothing more than to reach into his head and scratch them like a cat attacking a catnip-infested toy. He stood alone in the dark basement after turning off all the lights, lips quivering as tears rolled silently down his face. He wasn't one for crying, and this time was no different. He didn't get sniffles or the ballooning sensation in his throat that often accompanied a good sob session. Tears oozed out of his eyes beyond his control, as if his body insisted on crying with or without his blessing. His balled fist wanted to blast right through the wall while the other yearned to crash the baseball bat over someone's head. He tore back up the stairs, barged through the kitchen and family room, and stormed up the stairs to his bedroom where Erin remained sitting up in bed, looking as if she thought the floor was hot lava that would melt her body if she dared try to step down. "We need to talk," Brandon said sharply, leaning the bat against the door and plopping himself on the edge of the bed at Erin's side. Erin's eyes, already bloodshot, bulged a bit more. "Hear me out and don't panic, but I think someone is sleepwalking. There's been too much going on in the middle of the nights." He let his words fall to her ears like a feather swaying to the ground. It took her a moment to process what he had said, her face scrunching into confusion. "Impossible," Erin eventually said, crossing her arms over her bosom. "One of us would notice." Her voice became suddenly awake, and Brandon figured he must have struck a nerve. He looked up to the ceiling and nodded, looked back down to Erin, and shrugged his shoulders. "Sleepwalking?" she whispered, more to herself. "Think about it. The lights, the running water, the car. None of it makes any logical sense. There has to be someone behind it all, these things don't just happen." Erin looked down to the bed in deep thought. "What do we do?" she whispered. "Well, I was thinking I can sleep downstairs, maybe throw off my body's sleeping patterns. I think it's me. You've been impossible to wake up and the kids aren't big enough to do the things that have been done." "Sleep downstairs? I don't understand how that solves anything." "I don't know anything about sleepwalking, but I figure changing where I sleep could throw things off, maybe help us figure out for sure if it's me or not." Erin pursed her lips and shook her head. "Then go. I think you're being a bit paranoid. But if you think getting away from me is what's best for you, then be my guest. I'd offer to stay awake and watch you sleep, you know, like a loving wife would do. You've been so emotionally detached these last few days, but you never bother telling me what's wrong. Maybe we could have figured this out together, but go on with your first solution and be by yourself downstairs." The words cut into Brandon like a chef's knife slicing into a Christmas ham. He frowned, unsure if he should respond. It had been his car whose lines were cut, not hers. It had been him who found the family room covered in all that fucking cotton. And while it had been Jordan's toy set on fire in the oven, it was Brandon who was home while it happened. When he was sleeping, of course. Erin was mad for all the wrong reasons. Brandon knew it was him, and he simply wanted to try and prevent it from happening again. Her sudden outburst caught him off guard, and he certainly didn't have the energy for an argument in the middle of the night. "Fine," he said, defeated, crossing his arms and letting the baseball bat drop to the floor. Resentment bubbled underneath his accusatory tone. "Fuck it all, let's just go to sleep. Nothing to see here." "Brandon!" she snapped, but he had already stalked out of the bedroom and stomped down the stairs like a pissed off teenager. Brandon heard her let out a loud sigh before she slammed herself back on the bed. His hands were trembling, and he wasn't sure if it was from anger, fear, or exhaustion. Whatever the emotion, it didn't leave when he reached the main level, and continued with him as he rushed down the stairs to the basement. Worried he might literally lose his mind if he didn't fall back asleep, Brandon sat on the stool behind their bar, pulled out a bottle of rum and a Colorado Rockies shot glass, and poured himself a shot. Then another. And another. Then one more for good measure. He returned upstairs immediately, sure to get back to at least the main level before the alcohol kicked in. He made it with no problem and collapsed onto the couch for the rest of the nigh

Chapter 13

DECEMBER 19

B randon enjoyed his best night of sleep in a while. He had drunk just enough rum to knock himself out cold. When the sun broke through the kitchen window and illuminated the main level, he moaned and rolled over, slightly dizzy. Nemo had snored along with him all night, but had already gone outside through the doggy door. Brandon rolled off the couch at six, stretching, his joints popping and cracking as he reached above his head with outstretched arms. The sound of Erin's soft snoring trickled down the stairs, as if mocking him for throwing such a childish fit last night.

You think you can prove a point by sleeping on the couch? he imagined Erin saying. Well, then, watch me have the greatest night of sleep of my life! The truth was, Brandon enjoyed the rare nights alone on the couch. In solitary, his mind was clear and focused, able to absorb the world around him. We both slept great, and that's all that should matter. I still love you, and you love me. Now let's move on with our lives. He dragged himself into the kitchen, eyes bleary, breath sour, and flicked the switch on the coffee maker. It hummed to life as he leaned against the counter, unsure if he was still tired or possibly hungover. Four shots shouldn't have been enough to feel an effect in the morning, but crazier things had happened in the world of late-night alcohol. Once his mug was filled, the fresh odor of coffee overloading his senses, he took a sip before shuffling to the back door to check on Nemo's water jug outside. It appeared just about empty, so he slid open the door and stepped out to the cool morning to grab the container. Snow covered the backyard in random patches, nothing remaining on the slab of concrete that served as their patio. The grass, where it showed, was dormant and yellow, appearing as if it might catch fire from the simple flick of a cigarette. The weather had been below freezing over the past week, but this morning already felt much warmer, maybe preparing for a day in low-40's. "Nemo!" Brandon called out once his four-legged friend didn't come running around the corner. He whistled and slapped a hand on his leg before turning back into the house with the empty jug. He filled it in the kitchen sink, keeping an eye out the window for Nemo, and worrying when he still didn't appear after a whole minute passed. He always runs toward the door when he hears it open. Always. The backyard seemed extra still, deadly silent, when Brandon returned with the jug of water. No birds chirped, no car motors grumbled by, and no breeze whispered through the snow-covered trees. All Brandon heard was the sound of his own breathing, hollow in his ears. "Nemo?" he called out, a nervous crack in his voice. His heart raced as he thought the worst. The snow and wind from the past week could have damaged the fence and left a gap for Nemo to squeeze through. The snow had finally melted enough to reveal this opening to the dog, and he surely escaped, wandering through the neighborhood without food, water, or warm shelter. He wouldn't last in the wild for a single one of these frigid nights. "Nemo?" His voice wavered, and Brandon took a brief step inside to slide into his outdoor shoes he kept next to the door. Grass stains and mud caked their surface, as he wore them to complete yardwork. He slid the backdoor closed and trudged to the side of the house, calling out Nemo's name with every couple of steps. The concrete gave way to frozen, hard ground. Grass crunched beneath each step as he avoided the patches of snow. On the side of the house they stored their camper, covered up for the winter months, waiting to be let back out into freedom come spring time. The cover was solid gray and draped from the top to the side, barely scraping the ground. A dark splatter like mud appeared on the bottom edge of the cover. He took one more step before realizing it was blood, freezing him where he stood, heart trying to rip through his ribcage. "Nemo! Come here right now!" His voice wavered as he attempted to sound authoritative. A car zoomed by well too fast for driving in a neighborhood, and the roaring engine made Brandon jump, briefly snapping him out of the trance he had fallen into from staring at the bloodstains. Nemo didn't come and Brandon was forced to approach the camper, the splatter growing bigger, darker, and deadlier with each step. After the car had driven off into the distance, he was once again left in a deafening silence. He reached the camper and squatted to examine the stain. It was certainly fresh, a handful of the droplets streaming downward like condensation on the bathroom mirrors after a steamy shower. A lone streak of blood, no more than a centimeter wide, oozed from beneath the cover, running into the dead grass. Brandon reached his trembling hand to the cover and gripped it firmly between his fingers, taking a deep inhale before swinging it up to reveal what lay behind it. "AAAHH!" Brandon wailed, lunging backward and falling on his ass, rolling into a pile of old dog shit that had collected on the lawn over the past few weeks. The cover fell back on top of Nemo's head, revealing his shiny black nose, lifeless brown eyes, and mutilated neck. Blood caked his fur as he lay limp on the slab of concrete. His tongue hung out of his mouth like a dead worm, bright pink in contrast to the pool of blood it was dipped in. "No, no, no," Brandon muttered, tears streaming from his eyes and blurring his vision. The cover concealed the rest of the dog's body, so he wasn't sure what exactly had happened. With a numbing rush of adrenaline, Brandon scrambled back to his feet and flailed toward the camper, lifting the cover with the caution of someone opening a hidden treasure chest for the first time in hundreds of years. The sight sent an instant gag into Brandon's throat, staying there and ballooning as he witnessed the bloody scene. Nemo's head had been separated from his body, hanging on by nothing more than a chunk of pearly white bone that appeared to be his spine. The throat had clearly been chewed through by a creature with sharp fangs, his furry flesh shredded like beef brisket, dangling in flabby chunks. "Jesus Christ," Brandon cried. He kept his eyes locked on the family dog, physically unable to look away despite his brain's demands to do so. His throat had clenched to the point he couldn't so much as swallow his own spit. The cold air stung his lungs with each difficult inhale. All of the drama from last night seemed a thousand years in the past. Something had viciously attacked Nemo, and they were all fortunate that whatever it was decided to not take a stroll through the doggy door into the house. He finally dropped the cover from his grip and dragged himself inside. Erin had to see before he started digging a grave in their backyard, so he went upstairs with heavy, depressing steps, the world spinning as the shock of the situation struggled to settle. He had lost track of time, but found Erin in the bathroom, dressed in her robe and crouched over the sink as she washed her face. "Hey," he said, the lone word forced out with all his might. Erin locked eyes with him, but didn't say anything. "Something's happened," he said next, his voice cracking as his lips quivered. Erin's cold stare immediately softened into a look of concern. Brandon rarely cried, so she quickly understood that something wasn't right. "What is it?" She lunged through the doorway and grabbed him by the arms, which were also shaking. "Nemo's dead," Brandon said, flat and forced. Erin stepped back, releasing his arms, and met his eyes once more, this time to confirm that what he said was indeed true. Brandon's face turned red and scrunched into distortion as he nodded. "It's so bad," he wailed as he buried his face into her shoulder. Erin rubbed his back while still processing what had happened. "Something killed him," Brandon managed to say between whimpers and sniffles. "Something ate him." Erin's eyes welled with tears as she pushed Brandon off her to see his face. "What would eat him in our own backyard?" Brandon shrugged. "Whatever it was almost ripped his head straight off his body." Queasiness filled his stomach as the image of Nemo's dismembered body remained crisp and vivid in his mind. "Do you want me to go look?" Erin asked, her tone suggesting she'd rather do anything else. Brandon shook his head. "Only if you want to." Part of him hoped she would go see the damage, just so he didn't have to be the only one with the gruesome scene stuck in his head. "I'd rather not," she said. "I'll get the kids up and let them know that Nemo is no longer with us." Erin spoke in a lifeless monotone. "You're going to bury him?" Brandon nodded before pulling Erin back into his embrace. He couldn't even remember what their argument had been about last night, and at this point it didn't matter. They remained together in their bedroom for another five minutes until Brandon regained control of his breathing. "Okay, time to get this done," he said, more to himself. Erin leaned in and gave him a kiss, tears running down her cheeks. "I'm sorry you have to do this." "Me too." Brandon returned downstairs and grabbed a trash bag from the kitchen before heading to the garage for a shovel. Before he started digging, he sent off another text message to his boss to let him know of today's tragedy. The frozen ground resisted the shovel with every strike, mocking Brandon when he'd slam the blade to the ground, only to have it bounce back and send a nasty shockwave through his body. He would dig for a good ninety minutes that morning, oblivious to the little gray eyes watching him through the kitchen window.

Chapter 14

DECEMBER 20

With Nemo dying on Thursday morning, Brandon was told to take the rest of the week off. All of the events that had happened so far now seemed irrelevant and petty. Brandon forgot all about haunted spirits or sleepwalking. Nemo's death struck the family hard, and they all needed time to mourn the loss of the dog they had since moving into the house over four years ago. Riley struggled to cope, crying at the news, and bawling a flood of tears when Brandon walked her outside to show her Nemo's new home beneath a circle of rocks used to cover the grave. Jordan didn't quite understand, but clearly sensed something had gone wrong. Erin had called the city's animal control to report the incident and inquire about what may have done such an atrocious act. They informed her that both coyotes and foxes had been spotted in the neighborhood, but only a coyote would likely attack a dog. They tried to resume their lives as normal on Friday morning. Erin and the kids were off to their final day at school and daycare before Christmas break commenced. Brandon stayed home, weary and emotionally drained. Digging a grave in the bitter days of December proved physically difficult and mentally grueling, especially considering why he had to dig a grave. After seeing the kids and Erin off, Brandon spent most of the day walking around the house like a zombie. He'd start a simple task, like making toast for breakfast, only to find himself distracted and unaware of his surroundings. The toast had popped, yet he stared out the kitchen window to the fresh grave, pondering what the hell had happened to poor Nemo. Brandon noticed Snowball sticking out of one of the Christmas stockings hanging on the family room mantle. Even with all this, Erin still keeps him moving around. He had forgotten about the silly tradition with Snowball, too consumed with hanging on to the last threads of his rationality. Yet there he was, watching with those sideways eyes, his crooked grin hidden beneath the top of the stocking. Brandon eventually ate his toast, washing it down with a glass of milk, and proceeded to the couch for a full day of lying down and watching TV. Normally he'd complete some tasks around the house that always seemed to get put off, but he needed a true day of nothingness. He would flip through the channels for something familiar, and planned to doze in and out of different naps throughout the day. Maybe he would get up for lunch, maybe not. The day had zero plans and he fully expected to keep it that way. Brandon fell into a trance watching SportsCenter, his mind still unable to focus, being tugged a different direction. Regardless, he kept his eyes on the TV screen, and worked his hardest to concentrate on the sports highlights. He watched for an hour, the time passing feeling more like a week, and by the time nine o'clock rolled around, he was ready for a morning nap. "Brandon," a voice whispered, high-pitched, and somewhat childish. "Psssttt!" Brandon didn't flinch, too exhausted to move, and instead muted the TV. "Brandon," it called again, clearly coming from the fireplace. His brain continued trying to fall into sleep, and he thought maybe he was already dreaming. "Wake up, you chickenshit," the voice called out, and this made Brandon sit up stiffly, gawking to the fireplace's dark pit as his hands balled into fists, ready to fight whatever might come out. "Up here, dumbass." Brandon's eyes wandered up and locked with Snowball. The elf's stare was no longer sideways, his eyes meeting Brandon's straight on, wide grin remaining as it always had. This isn't happening, Brandon thought. No, sir. You fell asleep and are dreaming. That's the only possible explanation. Brandon stared at the elf, waiting for it to say something else, but it stayed quiet, spreading relief that it was indeed a dream. After a minute, the elf giggled. It didn't move, not its mouth nor body, but it certainly giggled like a child. Thank you for the delicious breakfast yesterday morning, its voice continued. Brandon watched the elf, not believing his eyes, or his ears, and accepted the harsh reality that he was now officially mentally insane. "That's all this is," he said aloud. "The sleep deprivation. The constant paranoia. All capped off by seeing Nemo shredded to pieces like a stuffed animal. I've snapped. A nervous fucking breakdown!" Snowball howled a laughter that could only come from deep within his gut. *That's a good one*, he said, his voice only present in Brandon's head, or so it seemed. *And here I am thinking I was the only crazy one in this house. Good to know you're on my team, Brandy Boy.* Brandon's late grandfather used to call him Brandy Boy, and oh, how he hated that nickname. As a child it drove him crazy being called what he considered a girl's name. There were no boys named Brandy, and it always embarrassed him when his grandfather called him this in public or in front of his friends. It was a name he thought he'd never hear again, and hearing it come from the elf's mouth—or from its mind?—felt slimy, like tree sap stuck on his hands that he just couldn't wipe off. He debated speaking back to the elf. So far he hadn't, convinced doing so would be the nail in the coffin. Call in the men in whitecoats, folks, Brandy Boy is talking to the toys! He wondered if people who developed mental issues later in life even realized it was happening. Did they just carry on with their lives until someone, whether it be a family member or a county judge, decided it was time for you to enter the loony bin? Did one's sense of reality and normalcy just vanish one day, or was it a slow, silent leak, like air seeping out of an invisible hole in a tire? Was it possible to actually know and accept that some form of mental insanity had planted itself in your brain, and all you could do was hang on for dear life, praying and hoping it will go away on its own? I am not talking to this elf, he thought. There's no reason to, because he's just a toy. Erin bought him in a store to play a fun game with the kids. He's not talking to me, and I'm not going to talk to him. The elf kept its cheesy grin as Brandon mentally worked his way through this situation. You'll be gone in five days. Christmas Eve I will personally pack you away, and just maybe we'll "lose" you. To the dumpster where you belong, you creepy piece of shit. Oh, Brandy Boy,

Snowball said, Brandon now convinced the toy was speaking telepathically. You can throw me in the trash, but I'll come right back. Hell, you can throw me in the fireplace if you wish, send me into a blaze of glory. But I'll come back. It might take me a little longer to piece myself together, but I'll always be back, until you're nothing but a pile of maggot shit in the ground. Brandon grinned at the elf, partly delirious, partly embracing his pending lunacy. Real or not, life would never be the same after this encounter. "I'm okay," Brandon said to himself, standing from the couch on wobbly legs. "No one is talking to me." He shuffled around the coffee table, determined to prove that this was all make believe. The elf was propped out of the stocking, red hat limp, and Brandon crouched over, his face mere inches away from Snowball. So close I could just reach out and give you a kiss! the elf's voice said within Brandon's head, causing him to scream and jump backwards, tumbling over the coffee table that struck the back of his knees. His arms flailed as his body soared over the table, spinning until it collapsed back on the couch he had just evacuated.

"What the fuck?!" he growled at the elf. Sanity be damned, that elf spoke to him, and he could no longer hold back. "Who are you? What do you want?" The elf didn't say anything for a moment, and Brandon was ready to check himself into the mental institute, but he finally responded in the cheery, devilish voice. Oh, Brandy Boy. I'm Snowball, and you should know that – you all named me. Brandon's chest heaved as he stared at the tiny monstrosity, his mind coping with an unfamiliar crossroads of deciphering reality versus absurdity. "Fuck you!" Brandon shouted, whipping out his hand to snatch the elf from the stocking, yanking him out and ripping the stocking off the mantle in a swift motion. "Go to hell!" He hurled the elf across the room, sending his cotton body into the wall with a crash. His entire body trembled with terror, and he felt his face flush a deep red as blood rushed in every direction. Is that all you got, Brandy Boy? You know I'm a doll—I don't feel anything. The elf giggled in a cunning way that sent chills up Brandon's spine. For a brief moment, Brandon feared that Snowball would keep on talking, right until he convinced him to climb on top of the house and jump, breaking every bone in his body from the neck down, leaving him a paralyzed mess. "Enough!" Brandon barked, storming into the kitchen and retrieving a plastic grocery bag from under the sink. He returned to the family room where the elf remained on the ground, his little legs in the air above his head as he lay upside against the wall. Brandon wrapped the bag around his hand and crept toward Snowball, his hand open like a claw as he crouched down to pick up the elf like a piece of dog shit in the backyard. Hehehehehe! Snowball laughed as Brandon picked him up, and turned the bag inside out to seal the elf within, tying a knot with forceful, good measure. "You're done, you piece of shit," he spewed through gritted teeth. With a death grip around the bag, he trudged out of the house, jacketless in the blistering cold, but the rage kept him plenty warm. Most of the snow had melted away, leaving scattered patches where the sun rarely hit the lawn. He flung open the wooden gate on the side of the garage, tossed up the dumpster's lid, and slammed the bagged elf to the bottom with a hollow thump. "Rot in hell!" he snarled, stumbling away on legs swollen with adrenaline. Snowball didn't speak again, nor did he laugh in his hellish way. Brandon returned inside the house, relieved that it was finally quiet, yet terrified that he now had to deal with his broken mind.

Chapter 15

DECEMBER 21

Brandon had spent the rest of Friday brainstorming lies about where Snowball could have gone. Maybe the kids had gotten a hold of him and misplaced him among their toys. Perhaps Nemo's ghost took it as a chew toy. Maybe he just got up and walked off, because toys came to life, right? The kids were the only realistic explanation that might work, so he decided to go all-in with that story. "I haven't seen the elf," he recited to the empty house, feeling a return to normalcy now that the teasing little toy had finally been silenced. Was it possible to experience a manic episode toward a specific object, and resume life as normal once it was gone? Even if the elf's voice had been in Brandon's head, it ceased after he threw it in the trash. Surely that wasn't a coincidence. Once the kids arrived home, he had managed to push the elf to the back of his mind, and allowed himself to enjoy the evening. They went out for dinner to a local pizza joint, and picked up a movie and ice cream for Brandon and Erin to watch later that night. Brandon's mind felt cleansed from the elf, as if he were a distant memory and not a discarded toy lying at the bottom of the dumpster. His conscience was so clear, in fact, he went to bed at eleven and slept the entire night without interruption. * * * He woke up Saturday, not to the banging on the walls or a possessed elf doll, but to squealing kids climbing onto the bed and jumping on him and Erin. He didn't feel that instant tug of fatigue that had started to accompany his every morning, instead refreshed and ready for the weekend ahead. A fresh blanket of snow had dumped overnight, only an inch, but enough to make outside a blinding blanket of whiteness. With four days until Christmas, Brandon thought the scenery was perfect for a quiet Saturday at home. He made breakfast while the kids watched cartoons in the living room with Erin, plugging in his headphones while he prepared eggs, bacon, pancakes, and toast. Once the table was set, the kids rumbled to the kitchen table, Riley climbing into her chair, Jordan standing beside his, waiting for someone to lift him up. No one had brought up Snowball, and every minute that passed, Brandon grew a little more anxious at the unavoidable question of "where is Snowball this morning?" The question never came, and by an unfortunate stroke of distraction, Brandon was off the hook for the immediate future. They settled in, devouring the full course breakfast in a matter of minutes. Once the kids finished and returned to the cartoons, Brandon and Erin stayed at the table, discussing the day ahead, debating if they should head out for last-minute shopping or save it for tomorrow. A thunderous knock came from the front door, startling Brandon and Erin as the kids squealed and ran back into the kitchen to their parents. "Everyone calm down, it's just someone at the door,"

Brandon said, sliding off his chair and shuffling through the kitchen. As he started down the hallway toward the front door, he saw two figures swaying side to side through the window. A closer look revealed them as a policeman and policewoman. Brandon's stomach sunk, his mind running through thousands of possibilities as to why the police would be knocking at his door on Saturday morning. He pulled it open, hoping for the best. "Good morning, sir," the male officer said, brushing his gray goatee, blue eyes beaming at Brandon. "I hope we're not interrupting your day." "No, officer, how can I help you?" Brandon asked, fighting off the tremble trying to creep into his voice. "I'm Officer Yates and this is my partner, Officer Ramirez. We just have a few questions for you, Mr. Armstrong, if you don't mind." Brandon looked around the neighborhood and felt a lump form in his throat when he saw the county coroner's van parked next door, a handful of cop cars splayed across the street with their lights flashing. "Sure. What's going on?" "Mr. Armstrong, were you home last night?" Officer Ramirez asked, her wide brown eyes studying Brandon like a hawk. "Yes, my family and I were all here." "Do you have any security cameras on the outside of your house?" "I don't. Can you please tell me what's going on?" Officer Ramirez pursed her lips and looked to the ground before returning her gaze to Brandon. "Your neighbors were found dead this morning." She nodded her head next door where all the commotion had gathered. "We're not sure if it was murder or not," Officer Yates said. "We found them quite mutilated, almost as if an animal had attacked them. But we found zero traces of animals in their house." "The Wagoners are dead?" Brandon asked, his hand subconsciously moving over his mouth. The Wagoners were an older couple, pushing their eighties, who always offered a warm smile and greeting whenever they crossed paths. Lucy Wagoner brought over a fresh pumpkin pie every Thanksgiving, and Donald sometimes shoveled the sidewalk while Brandon was at work for the day. "It's no issue. I was once young with two little kids, I know you don't have time to shovel," Donald had once told him after Brandon brought him a six-pack of beer as a thank you. The two families always looked out for each other, collecting mail while the others were out of town, borrowing a splash of milk when Brandon and Erin ran out in the middle of the night. "I'm sorry to say they both passed away," Officer Yates said. "There will be an ongoing investigation for the next few days. It will take some time to sift through all of the potential evidence. "You didn't see anything out of the ordinary last night?" Officer Ramirez cut in, less sympathetic. Brandon shook his head, sensing Erin and the kids creeping down the hallway behind him. "Have there been any different people you've seen at their house recently?" Brandon looked up to the depressing gray skies, racking his mind for the slightest memory of unknown people visiting the Wagoner house. He shook his head as he crossed his arms. "Thank you for your time, Mr. Armstrong," Officer Yates said, reaching into his pocket to pull out a business card. "If you think of anything, or see anything suspicious, please give me a call." He handed over the card, pinched between two thick fingers. "Officer, can I ask . . . how it happened?" Brandon didn't really want to know, but a distant voice in his head—Snowball's voice, perhaps—

demanded he find out this bit of information. *Please don't let it be what I think.* Officer Yates cleared his throat before speaking in a lower tone. "Between us, it looked like a mountain lion attacked them. Their throats looked like some creature chewed them right out, but there isn't a single claw mark or anything else on their bodies, and that's why we believe it had to be a person." That chilling, devilish giggle echoed in Brandon's head, and he wasn't sure if it was real or part of a lingering paranoia. His brows furrowed and he looked to his feet. "Is something wrong?" Officer Ramirez asked. Brandon shook his head. "It's probably nothing, but our dog was just killed a couple days ago. His throat was shredded to pieces, but animal control told us there have been coyotes in the neighborhood." "Interesting," Officer Yates said. "Have you seen any personally?" "I haven't, but I had to bury my dog after finding him dead under our camper. It was . . . a bloody shit show." "We'll look into that, anything is possible at this point of the investigation. Thank you again for your time." Officer Yates tipped his hat to Brandon, and Officer Ramirez offered him a nod as they turned and walked away. The screen door fell gently shut as he watched them cross the street to a different neighbor's house. He turned around to see Erin with the kids hanging on to each of her legs, tears running down her cheeks. "Are they really . . . ?" Brandon nodded, causing her hands to slap across her mouth as she let out a sorrowful yelp. "I guess it happened last night," he said. "What happened, Daddy?" Riley asked, lunging toward him. Jordan followed behind her, hands held outstretched beside his head as he ran. "Mr. and Mrs. Wagoner had an accident next door," Brandon explained. The kids had no experience with death, and he wasn't quite sure how to talk his way out of this corner. "Can we go help, Daddy?" Riley asked, her big brown eyes daring her father to say no. "I'm afraid we can't, sweetie. The cops are there and are taking care of everything. We just have to wait here and let them do their job." Riley's bottom lip frowned upon the rejection, but she didn't seem too upset. "How about you kids go upstairs and play in your rooms for a little bit, okay?" Erin said, inching them toward the stairs. The kids cheered and bellowed before storming up the stairs. Once they were gone, Erin turned back to Brandon and bawled into his shoulder. He embraced his wife and tried to calm her down, but had a sudden urge to head out back and open the dumpster. All the answers to his questions would be answered with a quick peek under the lid.

Chapter 16

DECEMBER 22

The sensation of something crawling over his skin never left Brandon as he slid into bed late Saturday night. He had gone out to the dumpster after Erin collected herself, and what he found nearly made him vomit. After two minutes with his hands resting on the dumpster's lid, he finally swung it open to find the shredded remnants of the plastic bag he had wrapped Snowball in. There hadn't been anything else inside when he tossed Snowball in, and now the bottom of the container looked back at him as he peered inside. Oh, sweet Christ, please don't let this be true, he had thought, and repeated that same line within his head at least fifty times throughout the day. Their Saturday had been wiped out by the unfortunate news in the morning. Erin lazed around in bed all day while the kids played, fought, and napped in each other's rooms. The tragedy also led to no one asking about Snowball, providing a sliver of relief for Brandon during these frightening times. He tended to the family throughout the day, but mostly stayed on the main level, the TV on as background noise as he paced around in nervous circles. As much as the truth demanded to be spoken, Brandon couldn't bring himself to do it. It was too late, as far as he was concerned. He couldn't tell the police—or his own wife—what he suspected, because doing so would only make him appear guilty. Blaming a double murder on a Christmas tchotchke didn't end well for Brandon, regardless of how he tried to phrase it. He'd be seen as a schizoid having a nervous breakdown. But for him, it was now all clear. Consulting with the calendar hanging in the kitchen, he calculated back to when Erin pulled out their elf on the shelf, and found that's when everything started to happen. The busted car lines, the slaughtered stuffed animals, the running water. Everything. It was the elf. But it seemed to be coming for Brandon only. Nothing had happened to Erin or the kids, aside from being woken up, but there were also four victims to consider now: the Wagoners and the man who crashed into the front yard. And, of course, Nemo. Brandon closed his eyes and could hear that maniacal laughter in the shadows of his mind. Maybe I really have lost it. The brain can make things appear as desired. Maybe I've officially jumped off the deep end and this is now how I deal with tragedy— I blame it on toys. But where was Snowball? He did throw the elf in the dumpster, and there was not a way for him to get out. There wasn't a scenario in the world to explain where the hell Snowball had gone, short of someone rummaging through their dumpster. Maybe this whole thing has been made up since the beginning. Maybe there never was an elf and it's been part of my imagination this whole time. Brandon had many laughs by himself on this Saturday, even when he invited the kids to come downstairs and watch a movie, hoping it would distract him. Erin declined the offer and stayed in bed while he and the kids watched Zootopia for the hundredth time. The distraction never came, and for a moment, seeing the animals in the movie speaking and interacting with each other like humans made him feel queasy. His mind clouded with paranoia and terror, unsure how he'd ever be able to sleep again knowing that fucking elf was out in the wild, possibly wanting to hunt him down. The thought of this murderous elf roaming the neighborhood ate away at his psyche all day. He needed to tell someone, but doing so seemed too crazy. No one would believe him, not for a second. Erin came downstairs later in the afternoon, once the kids had finished lunch, and they had a somewhat regular day from that point on. She didn't bring up the Wagoners—and she wouldn't, not in front of the kids. They watched more movies as snow continued to fall outside, steady, but heavily accumulating. Brandon let his mind wander a few times, expecting Snowball to barge right through the front door and attack the entire family. Never in his wildest dreams, he thought. After dinner and once the kids were in bed, Erin called it an early night, explaining that she was too emotionally drained. Alone in the family room, paranoia swirling like the snowstorm outside, Brandon popped two sleeping pills before grabbing the chef's knife to take upstairs and stash in his nightstand drawer, sensing a baseball bat might not be enough if Snowball found his way back inside. He spent the next hour resisting the pills, his mind falling into darker depths. Look at yourself, he thought as he lay staring at the dark ceiling, the heater humming soothingly in the background. Sleeping with a knife to protect yourself from the little bad elf. Soon enough he'd have to explain himself to Erin if he kept bringing knives to bed. Surely it was a risk having the big blade somewhere accessible for the kids to grab, but the risk seemed less significant compared to what could happen if Snowball found his way home. Just ask the Wagoners. It wasn't until two in the morning when Brandon was woken by Erin's elbow nudging him in the ribs. "Check the heater," she mumbled, not really awake herself. As Brandon came to, he imagined he saw his breath as he exhaled, then quickly realized it was real, bolting up in bed, head spinning as the pills in his stomach clung to sleep, while every nerve in his body elevated to high alert. The house had turned into an igloo. The night called for temperatures in the single digits, and it felt close to that even from under the sheets. Erin's teeth chattered as Brandon jumped out of bed, off balance and wavering in the dark bedroom. He found their two bedroom windows wide open, freezing air pouring into their room. "What the fuck?" He immediately pulled open his nightstand drawer and grasped the knife's handle. Neither he or Erin would open the windows in the middle of a December night, which left one obvious suspect. "Snowball?" he whispered, bracing for that childish giggle to respond. But nothing came. He closed the windows in a hurry, darting across the bedroom and down the hallway to the kids' rooms, finding their windows had also been opened. Riley had buried herself under her sheets, but Jordan had not, his face frozen to the touch as his body shivered. Brandon slammed all of the windows, arms shivering from either rage or the falling temperatures gracing the inside of their home. He covered Jordan and sat on the foot of his son's bed for another five minutes until he felt his tiny body return to a respectable temperature. Brandon ran through the house, knife at his side as he closed all of the windows. Every single one had been opened, turning the house into an icebox. On the main level, he checked the thermostat to find the house's temperature at a chilling twenty-two degrees, nearly fifty degrees below what they had set the temperature to. The heater would now run all night, and he prayed to God it wouldn't break from overworking. He returned upstairs where Erin was now sitting up in bed, sheets pulled to her chin. "Why the hell is it so cold?" she snapped. "Every single window in the house was open. It's going to take a whole day for the house to get back to the temperature we want." Brandon now spoke with confidence, no longer fearing an evil spirit. He knew who—rather, what—was behind these acts, and was ready to hold the little shit ball accountable. Without revealing the truth to Erin, of course. "Brandon,

I think we need to move out," Erin said. "I don't like the things that have been going on." Brandon nodded his head as he considered this, hiding the knife behind his back like someone about to surprise attack an innocent victim. "That might be a good idea," he replied. "Or maybe we consult with a sleep doctor about the sleepwalking. Anything at this point." That topic had been pushed to the back burner, their argument shoved aside upon Nemo's death and never revisited. He rubbed his swollen, puffy eyes, his brain burning with exhaustion as the sleeping pills in his system demanded his return to bed. "Should we leave right now?" she asked, a high pitch creeping into her voice. "No. We'll be fine. I'll set up the space heater outside of the kids' rooms, and you and I can keep each other warm. I'll grab a couple extra blankets from the closet." His head bobbed forward as sleep continued its good fight over his mind. "Brandon, I'm scared." "It's fine. Everything is okay. I just went through the whole house. There's nothing to be afraid of." The words left his lips feeling fake as a plastic doll, but he knew better. There was plenty to be afraid of. "Lay down and try to fall back asleep, or it's going to be a very long night." It already had been a long night, and he had every intent on sleeping with one eye open. Somewhere in the shadows of the night Snowball was giggling, waiting to deliver his final present to the Armstrong family.

Chapter 17

DECEMBER 23

Jordan screamed a sharp, piercing sound that drilled a spike into Brandon's head. Nothing pushes you closer to insanity quite like exhaustion coupled with a shrieking child at one in the morning. Brandon felt drunk with fatigue as he tumbled down the hallway, praying to sweet Jesus in heaven that he wouldn't just open Jordan's bedroom window and toss the little guy out in the snow. Parenthood presents moments that test the very structure of one's mental stability, stretching sanity to its limits like a rubber band on the verge of snapping. Tonight was one of those tests. Shortly after they had dinner, Jordan's temperature climbed to 105.1, a number that terrified Erin into wanting to go to the emergency room. Brandon calmed her down and called the doctor's office, who informed them that the fever must be close to breaking, and as long as Jordan remained somewhat like himself, then there was no need to worry. Jordan was very much alert, crying every single hour since they had lain him down at seven o'clock. Every. Fucking. Hour. Brandon and Erin stayed in the family room watching TV until calling it a night at ten. The crying itself was easy to soothe—Jordan just wanted a calming hand on his back while he fell back asleep—but the repetitiveness drove both parents mad, alternating who would go calm him down each hour. It was officially the first hours of December 24, but nothing about the moment felt like Christmas Eve. At one point, perhaps three in the morning, Brandon started crying along with Jordan, rocking the toddler in his arms, wondering if he would ever get another complete night of sleep in his life. Jordan's body burned like a hot iron in Brandon's arms, sweat drenched through his Toy Story pajamas. He sneezed, spraying spit and mucus in every direction, plastering across Brandon's bare chest. That seemed to calm Jordan, as his wailing faded into a dull whimper, before he was snoring in a light sleep again. Brandon's eyes puffed out of his face, his brain melting with weariness, his body trembling from the lack of sleep. Jordan's fever had turned the night into a complete disaster. Snowball, sleepwalking, and haunted spirits were the furthest things from his mind. He only hoped to make it to the morning, and prayed Jordan would overcome the fever sooner than later. Christmas Eve was upon them, and with it, a hectic day of visiting family and preparing side dishes to take to Erin's family gathering that evening. A long day, and even longer night waited ahead, and soon, Brandon would no longer have to worry about Snowball.

Chapter 18

DECEMBER 24 (MORNING)

Jordan decided 6 A.M. was the best time to actually go to sleep. Riley played quietly in her room, instructed to do so if she ever woke up before her parents. She didn't enter their bedroom until nine, demanding pancakes. Brandon rolled out of bed since Erin had the final turn in putting Jordan back to sleep. Riley spoke at a thousand words per minute, telling him something about the pony situation in her bedroom, but he simply couldn't focus to keep up, nodding and mumbling as they made their way downstairs. The long night had already turned their day on its head. They didn't need to leave the house until two, but Erin had planned on waking up at nine to start the two side dishes for later that evening. The microwave's clock teased him as it glowed a time of 9:08, Erin still snoring upstairs where Brandon hoped to rejoin her after Riley finished her breakfast. He positioned Riley at the kitchen table so she could face the TV, turning it on and collapsing onto the couch as she ate, giggling between bites as she watched an old re-run of Tom and Jerry. The last three hours of sleep he had caught felt like heaven compared to the rest of the night, and he feared his body might be awake for the day now that he had gotten up and moved around the house. Instead, the TV lulled him into a daze, to the point he couldn't move because his body was so relaxed with his legs dangling over the arm of the couch, body tucked perfectly into the deep crevice. He could have been floating on one of those inflatable beds in the swimming pool if he didn't know any better. Just as sleep flirted with him once more, Riley called out from the table, "I'm done, Daddy – can you help me get down?"

He groaned as he used all of his might to stand up, assured by the fact that he was one step closer to returning to his cushy mattress and fluffy pillow. Riley climbed out of the chair and down his leg as he stood next to her for support, promptly taking her father's place on the couch to settle and watch cartoons all morning. "Sweetie, Daddy's going back to bed. Will you be okay down here?" She nodded, not breaking her stare from the TV. "Okay, me and Mommy will be upstairs if you need anything. Please don't go into your brother's room—he's sick, okay?" "Okay, Daddy," she said in a cheery voice. Brandon patted the top of her head before dragging himself up the stairs. Even with his mind feeling somewhat awake, the prospect of returning to sleep proved too tempting. Erin lay on her side, curled into the sheets, and Brandon slid back into bed, falling asleep within minutes. * * * Everyone else woke up shortly after noon. Jordan strolled into his parents' bedroom, climbing into their bed, smashing their limbs underneath the covers as he progressed toward the small gap between Brandon and Erin. He lay on his back and sucked his thumb without a word. Erin rolled over and checked Jordan's temperature with the thermometer kept on her nightstand. It was down to 102.2, their efforts of pumping him with fever medicine every four hours seeming to work. "We need to get up," Erin said groggily, unconvincing. "We don't have time to make sides. Just need to grab something at the store." Brandon moaned in agreement, still not quite awake enough to speak. "We go store, Mommy?" Jordan asked between thumb sucks. "Yes, little mister," Erin said, giving him a kiss on his warm forehead. She turned her attention to Brandon. "What is Riley doing?" "I served her breakfast and left her watching TV downstairs." "Should probably make sure she's okay." Brandon stretched before rolling out of bed and heading downstairs, each step creaking beneath his feet. The TV in the family room showed Looney Toons, but Riley was no longer on the couch. "Riley?" he called out. She apparently helped herself to a juice box, as it stood unattended on the coffee table. "Riley?" He hopped off the final step and snagged the remote off the couch to turn off the TV, leaving the house completely silent.

"Riley?" he called again. "Are you okay?" He turned and went to the hallway bathroom, finding it empty. Just as panic crept into his throat, he heard quiet snickering from the living room, as if not wanting to be heard. He followed the sound, finding a bucket of toys emptied and splayed across the floor, a stack of blankets on the couch with a deformed lump underneath. "Where's Riley?" he asked the room, watching the lump squirm beneath the blankets. Another giggle, muffled as he stepped forward and grabbed the edge of the bottom blanket. "Where is she?" Brandon swung the blankets upward, Riley grinning after being discovered, breaking into hysterical laughter. He couldn't help but join her, grabbing his stomach as he laughed. "I got you, Daddy!" she cried after the giggling died down. "Yes you did. Good job." His pounding heart started to slow with relief. She rolled off the couch and returned to her pile of toys, resuming with her princess dolls as if nothing had just happened. "Are you ready for lunch?" he asked her. "Peanut butter jelly!" she exclaimed. "Peanut butter jelly!" "Okay, relax. I'll make you a sandwich." "Thank you, Daddy," she said as Brandon turned for the kitchen, her innocent, loving voice still making his heart melt, no different than it had the first time hearing it. The trash and recycle bins had empty boxes piled on top of them, and Brandon decided to take them out to the dumpster before Erin came downstairs and griped about them once again. The holidays seemed to make her lash out a bit more than usual about the most petty of matters. He slid open the back door before hugging the stack of boxes, squeezing them against his waist to keep them from toppling over. Walking sideways to see, Brandon stepped outside, the air cold, but not as bitter as it had been the prior days. As he reached the edge of the porch, stepping down to the dead, crunchy grass on the side of the house, he dropped the boxes, all feeling in his arms vanishing in an instant. At first glance, he thought he saw an old doggy toy lying in the grass, but a closer look showed him the truth: Nemo's severed head lying in the lawn, his tongue hanging out of his mouth just as it had when Brandon discovered him dead under the camper. "Holy shit," Brandon barked as he dropped the boxes, staggering backwards as if the head would jump up and attack him. His eyes followed the trail of dirt leading from Nemo's head, fifteen feet back toward the corner of the yard where he had dug the grave days ago. The grave was completely gutted, the three-foot circular hole exposed, mounds of dirt piled around it in small hills. Brandon didn't want to approach the grave, but had no choice, taking slow, hesitant steps. He had wrapped Nemo in a plastic trash bag before burying him, and caught a glimpse of the black, shredded remains of that bag. The lump of the dog's body remained in the earth, only his neck visible, clearly chewed apart by something with sharp fangs. Brandon froze where he stood, unsure what to do. Should he tell Erin? Have her come take a look to make sure he wasn't hallucinating? Or he could just re-bury the dog—with the head, of course—and pretend that nothing happened. It was Christmas Eve, and something of this nature would only further derail the next two days even more than they already had been. Besides, she had booked a time with the sleep doctor, and something of this nature could lead to a more drastic response from her. "Snowball!" he shouted, looking around, knowing that little fucker had to be nearby. There was no coyote, no fox, no rabid, lunatic squirrel. Somewhere in this very neighborhood a possessed child's toy lied in wait, a murderous creature ready to pounce on any living—or dead—creature. Brandon couldn't break his gaze from Nemo's head, a tattered chunk of his neck bone sticking out from the back, like a perfectly polished white eyeball staring at him. The head itself could have been mistaken for a dead bunny in the grass, Nemo's fur bloodied in random streaks, the flabby, tattered flesh on his neck looking like a line of cold cuts at the grocery store deli. He gagged at the sight, grabbing his stomach in his first movement since approaching the grave, looking back to the house to confirm no one watched him. With a clenched jaw, Brandon stormed away, passing the spilled boxes as he crossed the yard to grab the shovel and a pair of gardening gloves from the shed. He returned a minute later, shovel in hand, determination in his heart. Snowball was waiting for him; he sensed it in the air like a bloodhound tracking a dead body miles away. Brandon slipped the gloves on as he stepped toward Nemo's severed head, and closed his eyes as he bent down to pick it up, its weight reminding him of the soccer ball he kicked around the yard with the kids. He held the head in front of him like a pot of boiling water, running back to the grave and dropping it into the hole with a dull clump! as it hit the earth below. Nausea clawed into his throat, but he managed to hold it down. The hard part was done, and he started shoveling the dirt back into place. It would take him twenty minutes, hopefully enough time for Erin to remain upstairs and not come down to see what he was doing. As he tossed dirt on the grave, Brandon pondered how to get rid of Snowball once and for all. He supposed setting the elf on fire, melting him into a pile of plastic and charred cotton, might be the only option. Or he could tear him apart limb by limb, scattering his remains across the state like a twisted serial killer might do. Brandon started laughing as he scooped the final remnants of dirt, insanity tugging on his mind, much like it had the day Snowball spoke to him. Erin never came downstairs, not for another hour, and Brandon had a new secret to keep buried. He returned inside, ready for Snowball, ready to continue his day as normal.

Chapter 19

DECEMBER 24
(EVENING)

Christmas songs played in the background, drowned out by the conversation of the more than thirty people present at the Perry residence, Erin's childhood home where her parents still lived. Their house was slightly bigger than Brandon and Erin's, providing plenty of space for all of the guests, food, and presents that were hauled in for the evening. Brandon had gone through the afternoon with a guilty conscience. Erin deserved to know what had happened, but the timing made it impossible to bring up in casual discussion as they visited family on Christmas Eve. Although stressed and exhausted, Erin remained chipper as the holiday festivities awaited. They had made a couple of stops before arriving to the Perry house, first to visit Brandon's closest aunt and uncle who were on the way, along with some of Erin's cousins who weren't too far off. The kids were dressed up as elves for the day, and Erin promised to show Brandon her Mrs. Claus lingerie later for one final time before packing it away until next Christmas. That promise was all he needed to get through a night with his in-laws, where the conversation always turned into a bragging contest, both men and women in the Perry family having no shame in discussing the successes in their life. Erin somehow made it out of the trees as a humble and grounded person. This was something she had never noticed until Brandon drew attention to it after their third Christmas together as a couple. She hadn't believed him at first, but after closer examination, learned the unfortunate truth that had remained camouflaged so well during the course of her entire life. Tonight, Brandon poured himself a whiskey and Coke, and tried his best to remain hidden in a corner of the living room, close enough to the kids and Erin to not notice him being antisocial. Christmas Eve was always an unnecessarily long night. Erin's parents bought the kids an unreasonable amount of presents, often times taking them over an hour to open them all. The sight of it made Brandon sick, so he tipped his cup back and let the alcohol settle his nerves. Erin's brother, Matthew, found Brandon in the corner while the kids opened presents. "How're things going for you, Brandon?" he asked, his black hair and beard perfectly manicured to complement the gaudy silk suit he wore. Here we go, Brandon thought, ashamed he had made himself appear too approachable. "Oh, I can't complain. Job's going well and the kids haven't burned down the house yet. I'll call that a win any day of the week." Matthew let out a fake chuckle as he raised his glass of beer in the air. "That's very good indeed." A brief pause followed as Matthew took a sip, and Brandon braced himself, feeling forced to ask, "How are you doing?" "Fantastic. The firm had a monster year—I brought home 800 thou, with another

400 going to the Cayman Islands, if you know what I mean." "Impressive," Brandon said, stroking his brother-in-law's ego. Matthew worked for a big law firm downtown, and never shied away from sharing how much they succeeded. "It is, and we expect to double those numbers next year. Just might get to take some time off and cruise the world." "I hope you do." They both knew attorneys didn't get time off, and shared an awkward chuckle before each sipping from their cups. Brandon chugged what he had remaining, devouring the remains with three aggressive gulps. "Well, I need a refill, excuse me." Brandon nodded to Matthew before disappearing through the crowded living room where a dozen relatives gathered to watch the kids open their presents. He trudged through the kitchen toward the dining room that had been transformed into a bar and snack station. Trays of finger foods scattered across the massive table, and the bar stood in the far corner. Erin's mom, Donna, leaned against the bar as she poured more wine into her empty glass. "Oh, hi, Brandon," she greeted him, brushing back her short burgundy hair. "Enjoying

the party?" "Yes, I sure am," Brandon said, stepping to the bar where a keg was hidden behind the bottles of wine and every hard liquor imaginable. "That's good. Erin was telling me about some of the issues you've been having at home. Sounds like some strange happenings." She pursed her lips and cocked her head to the side as if she was reading Brandon. Jesus Christ, Erin. You had to bring this up at the Christmas party? Really? "Yeah, strange indeed." He wasn't sure what else to say, and avoided locking eyes with his mother-in-law, now that she had been let in on their little secret. "Have you thought about setting up a camera to record while you're away or sleeping? Might be a good idea just to see what's going on exactly." Shit, Erin suggested that weeks ago and I never looked up the damn cameras, Brandon thought, but figured it didn't matter at this point. What good would it do seeing that little elf floating through the air, hovering above their heads as they slept? He knew it was the elf, and believed after Christmas this would all end. Just like the companion story says: Santa's little helper returns home to the North Pole after the big man drops off the presents. "Thanks for that, Donna, we just might give that a try." She nodded with a grin, sipping her wine. "You let me know. If anything, I have a priest who can come take a look. Erin said she thought it might be some evil spirits." "Did she really? She's never mentioned that to me." "You didn't hear it from me, okay? She thought you'd think it was a crazy idea." Drunkenly, Brandon let out a childish giggle, his jaw hanging open in a brief moment of shock. This whole time he and Erin shared a similar suspicion, and now he questioned everything. Did she also have these strange run-ins with Snowball? Did she also suspect, or know, it was the damned elf behind all of this? Was it actually possible for her to have had the same experiences as Brandon, only to keep it all to herself to not seem like a total lunatic? He supposed it was all very possible. He had done it, and managed to go over two weeks with growing, shifting suspicions. We often think we're the only ones going through a unique experience, when in reality the neighbor down the street is going through the same thing. Or in this case, his own wife. Brandon let out a long sigh of relief. Whether Erin ever came to him with her suspicions or not, he at least knew he wasn't alone. It was their shared, unspoken secret. "It's not the craziest idea," Brandon said to Donna. "But I should get back now, the kids were still in the middle of opening their gifts." "Oh, of course. I'll be right there, too." Brandon left his mother-in-law behind, rejuvenated as he returned to the living room where more people had gathered to watch the debacle of the six child cousins buried underneath spent toys, wrapping paper, and ribbons. Matthew had remained in the same corner, so Brandon avoided him, settling behind the couch where some of Erin's cousins were mid-conversation. Erin knelt on the floor to help distribute presents, and Brandon gazed at her, grateful to have her by his side, knowing he would never find anyone better on the face of the Earth. * * * When the party died down and the kids fell asleep on the couches, Brandon and Erin finally made it to their car and started to drive back home. Erin drove after Brandon confessed to having six drinks. It was 10:30 when they pulled into their garage and carried the kids up to their bedrooms. The cookies for Santa had already been left out, so Brandon ate them, grateful to get something in his stomach before heading to bed. He fought off hiccups and hoped Santa's glass of milk in the fridge would send them away for good. He debated bringing up Snowball to Erin, the liquid courage certainly made him unafraid to do so, but she had promised him a romantic night in the Mrs. Claus lingerie. Bringing up a haunted toy would surely end that possibility. Erin stomped down the stairs after tucking in the kids, four shiny presents held in her embrace, marked as gifts from Santa for each member of the family. Brandon made his way to the living room to help her set them up, but instead stopped to watch her glide across the floor, the Mrs. Claus skirt flowing behind her. His jaw clenched as he gawked at her bending over to place the presents under the front of the tree, her calves and thighs tight and bulging. Erin took a step back, examined the gift layout, and turned around to meet Brandon. "Hope you're not too drunk," she said. If he had been, he sobered up immediately as blood rushed to his crotch. She reached out for his hands, pulling him toward her body, planting her lips on his for a solid five seconds. When she pulled back, Erin turned away, keeping one hand's fingers interlocked with his as she led him toward the stairs.

Chapter 20

DECEMBER 25

Christmas never arrives with a bang. The clock strikes midnight while most are sound asleep, especially the children who most look forward to the holiday, and threaten to stay up late to catch old Saint Nick in the act, only to pass out well before eleven o'clock. There isn't some magical snowfall that commences to celebrate the official arrival of Christmas. Jesus Christ doesn't come parading down the street with the three kings, singing carols to wake up the neighborhood. The calendar simply flips to the next day, just like all the other 364 days of the year, but on this day, you wake up to presents and family in the warmth of a loving home. And even though no actual magic existed, a magical sensation still filled the air like invisible smoke. Christmas marks the closing of another year, celebrated with relaxation and true time off to unwind and eat and drink whatever the hell you like. Brandon felt all of this as he fell asleep, alcohol in his belly and sweaty sheets clinging to his skin. As he nodded off, he knew a heavy sleep was coming, all worries of the elf the furthest things from his mind. He hadn't seen the little bastard in days, and no one had asked of his whereabouts after distractions seemingly piled upon each other following the Wagoners' deaths. His bed was a cloud, and he was ready to drift away for the rest of the night on it. However, the night of Christmas Eve played by the same rules as any other night of the year. Any number of things can happen in the middle of the night to ensure you don't wake up in the morning. While this may seem less likely heading into Christmas day, the same odds applied as always. Brandon and Erin went to sleep that night with no worries about evil spirits or sleepwalking. Perhaps they were too distracted by their steamy lovemaking. They fully expected to be woken up by the kids, jumping on the bed to celebrate the arrival of another Christmas, demanding to go downstairs to see what Santa brought them. Sure, the gifts from Santa were under the tree, but no one would see them until Erin's parents let themselves into the house later that afternoon, after a couple dozen of unanswered phone calls to their daughter. The presents would remain untouched, the holiday cookies uneaten, the joy and laughter of the morning forever trapped in some alternate universe where horrific things didn't happen to happy families. Even if Brandon had the flicker of a thought about Snowball, it may have not changed the outcome of the night. After all, can you harm or kill something that's not alive to begin with? At one point in the last week, he longed to tear apart that elf, cotton limb by cotton limb, but Snowball never returned after his exile to the dumpster. Snowball was no longer the direct threat, though. The toy elf had bigger, more elaborate plans. Killing the old people next door provided no challenges. The old lady had zero chance after her husband gargled to death on his own blood. She never saw Snowball coming and likely had no idea what had wiped her off the planet in the middle of that fateful night. Brandon had his suspicions about Snowball, and Snowball knew this. The man was getting much too close to actually believing that the elf was indeed responsible for all the bad events happening in and around the Armstrong household. If he told the woman, it could spell bad news for Snowball. They'd at least put up a fight. Snowball had kept himself hidden on top of the camper after crawling out of the dumpster, and stayed there, waiting. Tonight was the night to make his move, for his powers would vanish once the sun broke the horizon in the early hours of the morning, gone for another year until the next lucky family stumbled across him in the holiday section at the local thrift store. The doggy door had been closed up, an unfortunate mistake, as Snowball had taken the dog too soon. Next time he'd play it smarter and leave himself an easier way to get into the house. Next time he'd make sure to not get thrown in the dumpster like some disgusting piece of trash. The thought enraged him and he couldn't wait to watch the man's throat get slit. Maybe he'd intervene and do it himself, but watching from a distance might be just as enjoyable. For now, Snowball hopped across the camper's roof, leaping to the house and climbing up the chimney like a stealthy squirrel. Not once during his time in the house did he see them use the fireplace, so he had no fear as he descended into the blackness. He felt no pain, therefore, let go of the chimney's edge, dropping through the darkness until smacking the brick landing in the Armstrong's family room fifty feet below. Dust clung to his velvet suit as he climbed out of the fireplace and started for the kitchen. He thought he had been so clever tipping over the knife rack, giving the man a hint of what was to come. Snowball scuttled toward the counter and leapt upward with unbelievable force onto the counter top, returning to the knife rack, its black handles nearly invisible in the night. He pulled out the chef's knife, yanking with all of the force in his tiny, cotton body. Now the hard part awaited. He and the knife had to get down from the counter without making too loud of a noise. Just because he could jump high didn't mean he could float. Snowball still abided by the laws of gravity. A rug lay on the floor below the sink, an obvious target to toss the knife, avoiding the potential amplified clash of it hitting the hardwood. He chucked the knife off the counter, hoping for the best. It made a soft, faint thud as it hit the rug, but nothing loud enough to be heard upstairs where the man and woman slept. Satisfied, Snowball slipped off the counter and landed on the rug in near silence. He only weighed one pound, mostly of cotton. He hugged the knife's handle in his grip, pulling it through the kitchen, the back side of the blade sliding on the hardwood as he lugged it down the hallway toward the stairs. He had done the stairs plenty of times, but never while toting something as heavy as the knife. Pure blackness swallowed the upstairs as he looked up to it, climbing onto the first step to begin his ascent. The furnace clicked on, the whoosh of warm air providing the perfect white noise in the background as he hurried up the rest of the staircase, the knife gently thumping on each step behind him. He reached the top after a couple of minutes, the man's snoring echoing throughout the entire floor. The grin that was permanently painted on Snowball's face now felt genuine as he approached the end of this journey. He peeked into the man and woman's bedroom, pleased to see both deep into their slumber. Any disruption at this point would throw the entire plan out of place. Snowball couldn't even lift this knife above his head, meaning he'd have to resort to biting if it came to it. He didn't enjoy eating the humans' throats. They had a salty, unsatisfying flavor; the dogs tasted better. The little people slept at the other end of the hallway, so Snowball hauled the knife in that direction. He reached the boy's room to find him sleeping upside down on the bed, splayed across the top of the sheets with his miniature thumb cocked into his mouth. Wakey, wakey, little boy, Snowball said with his mind, inching closer to the boy's bed. Climbing the bed was the last major hurdle to complete before setting the boy into the wild. Santa is here, little boy, do you want to go see him? Snowball climbed atop the bed, all but yanking the knife behind him at this point, and plopped down next to the boy's head. He kicked him in the face with his cotton foot, knowing it wouldn't hurt. Let's go, we have lots to do. Wake up, dammit! The boy stirred, took his thumb out of his mouth, and flipped over onto his stomach in a curled up fetal position. Wake up! NOW! This internal shouting seemed to do the trick. The boy flipped back onto his back, but now his eyes were open, slow blinking as they looked to the ceiling where a night light splashed an image of the planets. The boy didn't do anything besides stare, but Snowball knew he was getting closer. If he could just have the boy's full attention, he'd be able to possess him. Sit up! It's time to get out of bed. "S'owball?" the boy asked, slowly sitting up. Yes! It's me! Let's go play a game. Do you want to? The boy nodded his head, rubbing his eyes. "I play with S'owball." Yes! Let's play! Take this knife and go to your Mommy and Daddy's room. I'll come help you. The boy did as instructed, grabbing the knife from Snowball and climbing out of bed. He wavered once his feet hit the ground, clearly still waking up. Let's go! Snowball edged him on, leading him out of the room as he wobbled into the hallway. Follow me, and don't drop that knife. They shuffled into Brandon and Erin's bedroom, silence thick in the air between the man's snores. Let's go see your Daddy first, little boy. The boy obliged, walking along the foot of the bed with the knife held upright in his small fist, an arousing shade of evil filling his eyes as the elf infiltrated his young brain. Snowball was no longer a voice whispering in the boy's ear, but rather pushed his way to the steering wheel of the boy's body. They both tiptoed to the man's side of the bed, Snowball willing the boy to climb up the side, sure to keep the knife at a distance to not accidentally slice one of his own arteries and send this entire plan down the shitter. Okay, little boy, what we're going to do is simple. We're going to take this knife and carve your daddy's throat like a turkey. Got it? Then we'll do the same thing to your mommy. When we're done with your mommy, we'll take another stroll down the hallway and do the same thing to your sissy. Easy-peasy, and we'll be out of here in five minutes. The boy didn't say anything, but held up the knife in a steady hand, hovering the blade above his father's throat, Snowball in full control. Never realizing that snowball was not his friend and what he was about to do would change his life forever and make snowball a pramenet him.

The massacre in the Armstrong house remained a mystery long after the tragic events of that Christmas morning. Homicide detectives had no issue connecting the knife as the weapon used in the murders. The mother, father, and daughter all suffered similar fates: slashed throats in the shape of smiley faces. None of those three appeared to have put up a fight, let alone know what had even happened. A forensic team later confirmed that the three had died in their sleep. The little boy, however, was the only one of the victims not lying in bed. Instead, they found him face down in the hallway, the knife in his stomach, its pointy tip sticking out of his back. Theories swirled across the police department and the community alike. Once February of 2021 arrived, the police deemed it a cold case, not a shred of hard evidence to trace back to a potential suspect. With that announcement, everyone was free to develop their own opinions on what had happened that fateful night. Many in the neighborhood were struck with terror at the thought of a loose killer wandering the streets. They dubbed the unknown person as "The Santa Claus Killer," one of those twisted nicknames that seemed to glorify serial killers in hiding. The popular theory was that the killer had climbed down the chimney to enter the home. There wasn't a sign of forced entry. The topic of how the killer entered the house was the main discussion for weeks. Some speculated the boy must have heard a knock on the door and let the killer inside since he was the only one not sleeping upon his death. But that theory was promptly shot down, as the boy was only two years old, and the front door had a child-resistant lock on it. The neighborhood had suffered two sets of unsolved murders within a week, leaving the surrounding houses on high alert every night. Perhaps the killer was waiting for the paranoia to die down before striking again. Regardless, the neighborhood was never the same after that Christmas in 2020. The house remained abandoned, eventually put up for sale by the bank, but never getting any serious attention aside from an occasional ghost hunter or séance hoping to crack the code of what happened. Nothing had ever been reported as far as paranormal activity. There was never a light turned on inside, or a distorted shape standing at one of the windows like they expected after such a gruesome, unsolved multiple homicide. It was simply a cold, dark empty house, as if the family had gone to spend the winter in Florida. Various forensic teams cycled through over the winter, each hoping to uncover the overlooked detail that solved the case, but they only ever left with their heads hung low. Maybe some murders were supposed to remain unsolved, the truth known only to those who were there that night. In this case, the toddler had been the only one to see the murderer before having his own life taken, a secret that would remain buried with his casket in the ground. It wasn't until the summer when Erin's parents returned to the house to sift through all of their belongings, deciding what to keep, throw away, or donate. Family portraits and heirlooms were packed in a special box for them to take home, along with important documents to be shredded, and about one thousand dollars in cash. Clothes, toys, furniture, and all the little knick-knacks that made a home were piled into the living room for donation agencies to come and collect as they pleased. Erin's mother had a particularly hard time taking down the Christmas decorations that her daughter had so elegantly set up, a practice they had done together as Erin grew up over the years, not stopping until she had a family of her own. The decorations hit too close to home, and she had to stop in the middle of her intense sweeping of the house. She stepped away from the family room and returned to the kitchen to sift through the cabinets, and that's when she found the elf on the shelf, jumping back as his insane eyes and wide grin looked her directly in the face from atop a stack of ceramic plates. "Oh my God!" she gasped, laughing nervously once she realized what she had found. She grabbed the elf, thinking of how either Brandon or Erin must have hidden it in the cabinet for the kids to find, a new wave of sorrow swooning over her, consuming her in its dreadful grasp as she remembered when Erin had told her she bought the doll for the kids. They had been great parents trying to make Christmas as fun as it was supposed to be for their children. She tossed the elf onto the pile of things to take home, its lifeless eyes staring at the ceiling. Without her knowledge, it would eventually end up in the pile for donations, off to the next family who wanted to play the holiday's version of hide-and-seek. For now, it was merely a doll with a cotton body and crooked eyes, its grin cheery and welcoming, not showing a sign of the evil life that lurched beneath like a deadly shark waiting to prey on humans at the ocean's surface. The elf would hold that same facial expression for the months to come, waiting as kids went on summer break and returned to school in the fall. Waiting as they went trick o' treating for Halloween. Waiting as happy families stuffed their faces over Thanksgiving dinner. Waiting until Christmas returned, and with it, a new opportunity to unleash its evil upon the world.

THE END

About The Author

New York Times & International Best Selling Author Billie Dureyea Shell was born in Compton California and now lives in Ladera Heights with his wife and kids who he loves to spend time with. He is the Owner of several properties in the Los Angeles area and gives back to his community by providing low income housing to those who need it. He stated "It doesn't matter where you at or where you from it's what you do with your time. There's nothing you can't do if you put your mind to it".